Quixotic Erotic

Tamai Kobayashi

Quixotic
Erotic

ARSENAL
PULP PRESS
Vancouver

ARSENAL PULP PRESS
103-1014 Homer Street
Vancouver, B.C.
Canada v6B 2w9
arsenalpulp.com

The publisher gratefully acknowledges the support of the Canada Council for the Arts and the British Columbia Arts Council for its publishing program, and the Government of Canada through the Book Publishing Industry Development Program for its publishing activities.

Book and cover design: Solo
Cover photograph: Lucien Clergue/Getty Images
Printed and bound in Canada

This is a work of fiction. Any resemblance of characters to persons either living or deceased is purely coincidental.

"memory, need, and desire" originally appeared in *Piece of My Heart: A Lesbian of Colour Anthology* (Sister Vision Press, 1991) and *All Names Spoken* (Sister Vision Press, 1992).

"The Tale of the Time Traveller" originally appeared in *Getting Wet: Tales of Lesbian Seductions* (Women's Press, 1992).

"Egg" originally appeared in *Best Lesbian Erotica 2003* (Cleis Press, 2002).

NATIONAL LIBRARY OF CANADA
CATALOGUING IN PUBLICATION DATA:
Kobayashi, Tamai, 1966 –
Quixotic erotic / Tamai Kobayashi.

ISBN 1-55152-139-3

I. Title.
PS8571.O33Q59 2003   c813'.54   C2003-910383-8
PR9199.3.K59Q59 2003

Erotic

Quixotic

ACKNOWLEDGMENTS

A great thanks to all who assisted me in the creation and publication of this manuscript. No one writes alone and my debt is beyond measure. Thanks to my publisher Arsenal Pulp Press and those who have supported my writing throughout my career. Sil, you have been my friend for so long and through so much, what I say to you must be done over *mate* and some *dulce de leche*. My love to Esther, my fellow Capricorn; Linda, the smartest woman in the world; Hiromi, who taught me how to say "erotica" in Japanese; Ashok, who likes his martinis dry and ice down his pants; Aruna, ever patient with Gita, Maggie, and Ashok. My heartfelt appreciation to my "cover consultation committee."

Love to my crazy making family, as always, and to Toshi, thanks for the computer.

Erotic

Variations

She steps into the room, into darkness, the door closing behind her and turns, clicking on the switch.

Nothing.

Click click.

Damn light, she thinks, better call maintenance.

But she can find it in the dark, she is sure. And so she reaches, arms stretched out before her, her mind a clutter of spread sheets and reports. A supervisor's meeting at three, and where were those forms?

Dark, so dark.

Here, the table, her knees grazing the chair.

Her fingers. There. Fabric.

She steps back, confused. Her hand closing over – what? A sheet? No, her palm open, fingers spread against thread and weave – a shirt, and below, soft and full, a woman's breast.

God, I'm sorry, I didn't –

A whisper. Shhhh.

Stillness.

Why such stillness, she wonders.

But she can hear a rustling of air and cloth, closer now, a breath, feels a sudden thrill of danger, but no, it is a woman with her, in the dark. But close, the fragrant warmth, an intimate scent.

on a Kiss

Where is she? And what is she doing here?

Who –

Shhhhhh. Insistent.

She waits, confused.

Silence.

She will turn now, tired of this game. But feels . . . something. The ghost of a caress.

She shakes her head clear. The air is hot, too hot, and thinks, the ventilation in this building is terrible –

But again, a caress, like lips stroking her nipples.

Her breathing, harder now, fills the room. She swallows, a tightness in her throat, in her belly. Her head, spinning, where is the entrance? She is dizzy and that smell, intoxicating, and a hand, yes, to hold her up, her knees giving way.

But the hand. . . .

She can feel it, full, against her breast, a fondling, squeezing stroke, playful and tender, teasing and vindictive. She falls back, to the table, but the hand comes with her, the darkness, flailing, useless, her shirt falling away.

A mouth. On her nipple. And god, a tongue.

A gasp, torn from her own body.

Jesus what is happening.

Suck, stroke, suck, her ragged breath pounding in her head, a tongue rolling her nipple to stiffness, the devouring mouth, taking in, taking in, and last, a hard sucking pop –

She is free.

Cool air against her exposed breast.

Panting, she catches herself, the weakness in her knees, her back against the table. Her cunt throbs, a pulsing need as she locks her legs together, an electric shiver, this tingle, running up the groove in her back. She could stop this, a step to the door.

But – a hand cupping her other breast. Holding fullness, the weight and breadth.

And then there are the kisses, sharp, darting kisses, her cheeks, her neck, a tongue caressing earlobe and whirl. And lips. Such soft insistent lips. She presses against her, melting desire, her own hands, dancing, slipping through buttons, silky skin, frailty of bone, taste, a ring of bites along the breast, she holds a nipple on the tip of her tongue, takes into her mouth ripeness, wants to swallow.

The darkness, darkness.

She doesn't expect it, not a hand sliding down the front of her pants. She has never touched a woman before, never imagined. But the hand snakes down, feels the dampness through the panties, and balking, she jolts up and away.

What? What? A snapping panic, spinning vertigo.

Against the wall she catches her breath, feels the burning imprint of the hand, her own tell-tale weakness. Kisses, everyone kisses, she tells herself, but there, no. She's gone too far. This game has gone too far.

She shakes herself out of her dizziness, tries to visualize the room in the light.

Darkness.

She begins to move along the wall. Walls lead to doors, doors to freedom.

But that hand. . . .

She hits a corner, has she gone the wrong way? She thinks. The door should be directly in front of her. But one step out and she has lost the wall and she fumbles against the table.

The table, her palms flat against the surface. How did it get here?

She stops. And listens.

From behind her, arms encircle her, strong. Breasts press against her back, hips against her ass. A moan escapes from a mouth. Is it her own? The tumble of fabric, her belt undone, pants fall to the floor. She waits. The damp panties cling, her slickness betrays. Blood beats in her skull, between her legs. Does she want this? What happens now? Her cunt quivers at the thought.

Uncomfortable, she shifts, but a hand nudges her thighs open.

She waits. Hot, hot, her chest feels hot.

She feels the faintest trace of a fingertip, outlining her panties, a slow and deliberate delineation. She hears an intake of breath, feels a sliver of touch, realizes that she is nuzzling her, smelling her, spreading her. A breath blown against her wetness and she nearly cries, so close, so very close. Those hands begin kneading her ass, working the sodden cloth against the lips of her pussy, a chaffing delight. And she feels, what, as she clenches and unclenches her cunt? A tongue, no, quick, lightning kisses. She whimpers and suddenly knows that she wants this, this woman, this mystery.

Please.

A firm tug and the panties are off, a rush of air, a lingering breeze. Fingers and palm roam over curve of hips, she's pushed forward, stomach down, on to the table, her feet off the floor, footing lost, thighs open. She chokes, deliciously exposed. She grips with her arms, her hands along the edge.

And waits.

Feels, before she hears it. A tongue grazing the edge of her lips. The plip plop play of wetness between her legs.

She bites her lip, wills herself not to scream.

And the tongue spirals down, her tremoring thighs, the trace against the back of her knees, bites along the muscle of calves, strong calves, the delicate curve of ankles, frail bone, toes suckling arch a shiver. But hands, a sudden grasp, fullness of ass, tongue sliding up so deliciously slow, a groaning, curling ache from her slipsucculent cunt. Ah, a breath. Circling slowly, lazy and indolent, a clutch, as lips kissing vaginal lips, mouth sucking out the folds, in, out, and in again, beating out a rhythm that boils in her blood, deep and slow, a measured retreat, a reckless plunge, a tongue – then something – a finger dipping in, tongue slurping sweetness – she can hear it – a dance of tongue and fingers, a wriggling writhing torment of touch and touch, until –

Oh –

Two fingers. She feels the fullness, takes it inside of her, wants to hold, her pussy grabs, too late as the loss is wrenched out of her. Those fingers. In and out, thrust and retreat, it's the only thing she knows now, in the dark.

please god don't let it end

the viscid sound of fingers – out

please

breath slammed out of her

oh –

The scent, her own pussy juice dripping down her thighs.

In. Out. In.

She is inflamed, engorged, a rhythm building, a piercing need, she wants, god yes anything for this –

The door opens, a flood of light.

Blink. Blink.

Three fingers dive into her.

Shock, the storeroom and Reynolds has walked into the space. He's left the door open and light, light streams, catching the far wall, the distant table, chairs.

She can see me, knows who I am.

And Reynolds.

Her cunt contracts, but those fingers wiggle deeper.

But Reynolds has not seen her, not yet. He checks for his vials on the shelf next to the door, peering, the light from the hallway not strong enough.

She bites her lip, three fingers waving in her vagina, stroking her insides, goading her to come.

I am being fucked from behind in the storeroom. Please don't let him find me. Please god don't let her stop.

Reynolds pauses by the light switch.

Click click. And he is out the door.

The door snaps closed, and the fingers pop out.

Relief, yes, a ragged sob torn out of her. But quivering, her body begs for more.

She waits.

And waits. Cunt open and so willing –

Silence.

The arms come, enfolding her, a gentle rocking of hips against ass, a comfort. And a whisper.

Shhhhh.

Gently the woman takes her off the table, turns her, holds her.

She doesn't expect this tenderness, her tears, a sob catching in her throat. She does not understand these desperate yearnings, her frenzied desires. She kisses her, kisses her –

But the woman steps away.

The room, in darkness, whirls.

The lamp in the corner flickers on, casting a small pool of light. The woman, she can see her now, smooth brown skin, strong arms and curve of belly, the dark bush of pubic hair. Short, black hair. Beauty, beauty, could she have ever imagined this?

The woman comes forward, and she is suddenly aware of her nakedness, a fluttering shyness, even after this.

The woman. A whisper. I'm sorry.

Sorry?

I was expecting. . . .

And she realizes, sinking, the kisses, this joy, not for her, not for her.

Oh. The dryness of her mouth, the hollow of her stomach. Of course. She stoops, gathering her clothes, her body wailing against the loss. The air, a chill against her back, her shoulders.

But the woman watches.

Wait –

The woman guides her to the table, the lamp casting them in a different light, lifts her, barely to the edge.

The woman whispers, I want you to see this, how beautiful you are.

The lamp catches them, the woman kneeling, brushing back the thick hair of the mons, her fingers combing back the tangle, crinkly and damp. The woman gently nudges open legs, wider, a kiss to the navel.

She sees tongue darting out of the woman's mouth, such supple strength, wants her lower, deeper, her thighs twitching in anticipation. She is hanging on the edge of the table, muscles bearing down, juices trickling out of her, a droplet's caress. But the woman travels higher, licks the sweat beneath the breasts, areolas flushing dark. Will she stop to nibble, to tease, to suck? But no, rough bites into her chest, along the line of neck, and a deep clawing scratch along the length of her back.

She cries out, arching.

A shock, those nails.

The woman steps back. She can see her eyes, dark and veiled. Feather kisses, lips, and sliver of tongue.

The woman steps back, her hand reaches out to hold breasts, gently, her thumbs brushing lightly, agonizingly so.

Please – her legs jerk open as she gasps.

Ah, but I don't want to spoil my appetite, the woman whispers.

The woman drops to her knees, leans forward, spreads out

labia, unfolding those lips, the fleshy pinkness. Her breath is close, the vibrations of air as she smells her, heavy and musky, but the kiss is so slow, a soft sucking of the vestibule, humming, humming and then tongue, outside, between the curls and labia, the shaft rising up to the clitoris.

The woman is taking her time.

Lips, the woman takes them into her mouth, rolling, pulling, lapping up their sweetness, clinging dew, kneading her mound with cheeks, chin, the rubbing of nose.

On the table, her arms are shaking, legs quaking, giving way.

The woman cups her ass, holds her to this.

The vagina, not a hole, but a sanctuary, petals and petals, ridges and grooves, spiraling inward. She sips at the surface, suction pull, slurping sound – flicks at the brink.

Oh –

The woman, her tongue thrusts, deep.

And the woman can feel the cunt muscles squeeze, the desperate chase as she pulls away, thrusts deeper, and how she opens, how she takes, the woman presses her mouth into pussy, a kiss so deep she bruises her, rutting face, ravishing tongue. She wants to sink into her so deeply, but pulls, pulls away. The woman swallows the thickness, gulps the air.

The woman looks up at her. Whispers, what's your name?

Mariko, she blushes.

Mariko, I don't want you to come until I give the signal.

The signal?

Yes. The woman makes a gesture, two fingers, curling, a coaxing motion. Hold on, make it last. Make me work for it.

But how –

You'll know when you feel it. And the woman smiles. Such a lovely smile. But that mischievous tongue, playing along the clitoral hood, her mouth swallowing that little bud, a circular motion, a pulsing need. The cadence of her humming blood, Mariko can feel it, rising, an irreversible pitch, her hips bucking in rhythm, her own sharp cries and the woman's fingers sink into her, a stab to the core, in and out, that delicious sound of wet, she can't hold as mouth sucking clit and fingers curl, a beckoning come come come, scooping, as if to drag the orgasm out of her, shaking thighs, a cunt clutching gasp as she sprays, quaking, a shuddering release, a sob, even as the fingers ride out her pleasure.

A moment, and the woman holds her, Mariko collapsing forward but the fingers are still inside.

The woman smiles. You sprayed me.

Mariko blinks. She sees the puddle and blushes.

Sorry.

You ejaculated.

I didn't know I could.

The woman pulls her up, wipes off Mariko's tears. Didn't know you had it in you?

They smile.

The woman buttons up, all business now.

Mariko waits, a fluttering loss.

But at the door the woman turns. Same time, tomorrow?

Mariko nods. And the woman is out the door.

In

You sleep after a long day's work, and then a rally protesting police violence against the black youth of Regent Park. Dodging billy clubs and cops on horses, you've made your way here.

I can still smell the pepper spray.

Months before, you had fled the riot gear, for protesting poverty and homelessness, marching to Queens Park, linked arm and arm with other women and the billy clubs had met you there. You are on the coalition to stop racism and your back is hurting, knees still ache from a spill from your bicycle two summers before, and there are the Take Back the Night leaflets to be printed, petitions and pamphlets and signs.

You sleep.

My bed is too small for you, your dark skin darker against the ivory cream sheets. Our lives fit awkwardly, not the fairy tale, nor the lesbian feminist romance. We have to imagine ourselves anew, each and every day, your black Jamaican mother, Welsh–Irish father, my Hong Kong mah mah and Shin Ijushya otosan. In this too small bed, we try to be the world to each other and we know that this is not enough. We test each other, you and I, and mostly we fail. We bump and scrape and we bicker, at times fetishizing our differences, without exploring their meanings, enlarging them into fights that spill into the kitchen, the bathroom, the street. We

Sleep

fuck, and sometimes we don't, crying open our need on the table in the hall, bending over the pillows, staining the sheets.

You sleep.

I want to crawl beneath the covers, spread your legs, taste the saltiness of your pussy. I want to hear you moan and beg and curse and plead, to feel you shove your fingers into my cunt, as you push me beyond myself, somewhere beyond and within us both. When you sleep I can trace the contours of your belly, the tangle between your sturdy thighs. Your shoulders are so broad that my hands cannot encompass them, your back so long that I could take an eternity exploring. But we don't have the time. We never have the time.

I could say your kisses float like butterflies and your eyes are like stars, but I know the frailty of metaphors and the constellations are so far away.

When you sleep I wonder about your dreams. We never talk about the future. I can speak about globalization and the world economy, the exploitation of workers and the IMF, not as distant issues but as the concrete conditions of our lives. But when you wake I will crawl into the imprint of warmth that you leave behind, if only to entice you into the embrace of my thighs and I will kiss back the fears of tomorrows in this city.

So sleep, my love. I've made the pamphlets and rice steams in the pot. And when you wake I will hold you and we will dream together, of this time and place which claims and excludes us, the divisions which separate us, even as they make us whole.

Mirror,

S he knew she was watching.
But the mirror was in front of her and it had been so long
since anyone had touched her. Usually she would masturbate in
the dark, under her sheets, but lately. . . .

A few weeks back she had noticed the open curtains in her
neighbour's darkened apartment. Nothing unusual. But with her
mirror turned just so, she could see her. See her watching her.
Watching her when she came from the shower, towel thrown on
the bed, or dressing in the morning. At first she had thought it
was her imagination, or coincidence. But tonight she was sure. The
gauzy curtains did not hide her and the space between them was
so small. Now she would give her a full frontal view. She knew she
was watching. The mirror didn't lie.

She sat on the edge of the bed. Faced the window.

Earlier she had clipped her pubic hair. A few snips and she
had sculpted her bush, why she could even seen her lips, the
little hood. She gazed. Yes, she was watching, the devil even had
binoculars.

She turned on the lamp, shone the light on herself and slowly
parted her legs. Her vulva. Was she pleased? She spread her labia,
pushed out her hips. She remembered when she first saw women
exposed this way, in those cheesy magazines. Magazines of women

Mirror

spread in the most graphic way. Did women look like that in real life? No, too contrived, too obvious, those girls posing in those glossy sheets, too plastic, too impossibly perfect and all so white. But still she had stared. At those pussies.

As the woman was staring at her now.

She thought of the names for vaginas – beaver, cunt, hole. And a rose is a rose . . . but still so inadequate. The strangest word she had heard was pudendum, sounded like addendum, something tacked on, as an afterthought, in shame. The metaphors were better – caverns, gardens, the silkiness of orchids. . . .

She pinched her nipple, caught herself in a jagged gasp. Her thighs twitched wider.

She began touching herself, a circling caress, and sighed. What was it about masturbating that made women blush? Sometimes she would walk down the street and wonder, how many times has that woman come today? Does she fuck herself in the bathtub, the stream of water gushing over her clit, or rub her cunt over armchairs, plump and leathery, or maybe hardwood, with those stiff little knobs on the ends. Would that woman take a stranger's caress on a dance floor, or a quick finger fuck in a crowded steam room?

She bit her lip, her breath short and quick.

She thought of the women she worked with. Beth, with her roomy overalls, ample hips, what would it be like to nuzzle between her big, strong thighs? And Cem, she could imagine her pert, small breasts, those pink berry nipples, bursting in her mouth. Oh, she could feel slickness bubbling out of her.

She saw her watching in the mirror. Touching herself.

She slipped a finger inside, her back arching.

She loved this feeling, how the muscles engulfed her, surrounding, yet giving way, warm and sticky, her finger probing. She slipped in two fingers, swimming, the resistance of flesh, yet yielding, rippling with every motion, riding with every wave. She realized her hips were rocking against the pull of her hand, as if her cunt had a will of her own.

Oh god, the joy of fucking herself, and a woman watching from the window.

What was it about looking? What was it about being watched?

She took her fingers from her pussy. Sticky. Licked them clean.

Was she looking? Oh, she liked that.

She began rubbing her breasts, teasing out her nipples. She loved holding breasts, no matter the size, feeling weight in her palms, squeezing tender bite–sized buds. She dipped her finger into her cunt juice and smeared it on her tips, cool air against warm skin. She envied women who could suck their own breasts. If only she could suck herself, her cunt, she could fuck herself silly. She shivered at the thought.

She looked into the mirror. The woman had stepped forward, in front of the curtains. If she looked up, she could see her seeing her, touching herself as she stared through the binoculars.

No, let's see how far this game can be played.

She spread her legs wider, fingers swirling faster now.

She tried to imagine how she looked to her. Was she close enough to feel, close enough to fuck, her fingers sliding inside, yes, but oh, she wanted it deeper, fuller. She pulled her toy box out from under the bed, took out her vibrator, and, yes, her silicone dildo with the hand grip.

She looked at the mirror. The woman was not there.

Disappointed, but she was too far gone to stop. She set the vibrator on low and began with her thighs. Sometimes she would slide her vibrator into her tight jeans and walk around the apartment, the constant buzz a comfort, then turn it up until she couldn't stand it anymore and collapse on the floor. Once she had worn it to the bar, had danced with her hands jammed in her pockets and she'd come, leaning back on the speakers.

She slid the vibrator onto her clit and jumped, the pulse so intense.

She glanced back at the mirror. The woman was back, her clothes off. But she was still watching.

She put the vibrator aside and reached for her dildo, pushed her hips up so she could have a clear view. Lips parted, she slid it in slowly, teasingly, fullness and retreat. Did she like it?

She looked. The woman in the window had placed her foot on the ledge. The binoculars sat on the sill. One hand stroked her clit, the other held a candle which she guided into her pussy. She could see the other woman clearly now. If she looked straight through the window, they'd meet eye to eye. But the mirror. . . .

The mirror held her gaze. She could see the candle, not the best instrument, too thin for her taste, but as it plunged in and out, she could see the woman's pussy juices glisten down the shaft. Ah, they were stroking in tandem now. Is she fucking me, or am I fucking her, she wondered.

God, deeper, deeper, she wanted this so badly, couldn't wait any longer. Faster, her hand nearly cramping, faster, she grabbed her vibrator and pressed full throttle. She couldn't help it, that cry of joy as the buzz shot through her cunt, her hips bucked and twisted, the dildo plunging faster, god deeper. She moaned, window open, didn't care who heard, felt the beginnings of her coming, that wonderful anticipatory twitch in her cunt as she fucked deeper, faster, she looked, not at the mirror now, but the window, saw her, seeing her, both of them on the brink, ramming the candle in, juices sliding on silicone, vibration so deep, she fucked herself coming, a grunt rutting joy. Even as her cunt rippled and clenched, waves fell away, until, exhausted, she lay back on the bed.

♀

The videotape dropped in her doorway, no stamps, no address, a simple brown paper package. The binoculars were not what they seemed. And the woman in the window *could* see herself in that angled mirror. Sight travels both ways. The video: a woman fucking herself for a woman, fucking for the mirror, recorded on the viewfinder. But she was not alarmed. Written on the sleeve of the videotape, a name, address, and invitation. For a private screening. And a request to bring the box of toys.

They are lovers, working in the same office, but few in the company even suspect. Professional, courteous, and distant. Their coworkers think they hate each other. But one morning, during Shel's conference call, Junko comes into her office, pulls down Shel's lace panties and eats her out, tongue stabbing and then a full finger fuck. Shel is enraged. Plots her revenge.

The next morning Jun knocks on Shel's office door. She looks contrite, and for a moment Shel pities her.

"Can I come in?"

Shel nods. But this time it is Jun slammed against the desk, her pants down. Jun, already wet, had expected this oneupmanship. But Shel only slips something inside, an egg–sized something, and simply lets her go.

"That's it? That's all?"

"You've got a lot to answer for, the conference call, and fucking me on the photocopier." Shel hands Jun the xerox sheet, a grainy image of Jun's hand in Shel's cunt.

In the bathroom Jun sits on the toilet. What was it, this big surprise? She can't get it out, this egg, too round, too slippery, she is too wet for her own good. But it is time for her report and she steps out of the cubicle.

Shel is waiting outside with Sash, a new girl down on fifth.

Egg

"Looking for something?" Shel smirks.

Jun brushes past her without a word. But she catch's Sash's rebuke.

"Jesus, Shel, she's presenting today, give her a break."

♀

At nine–thirty, her report in front of the Board, with all the senior management in attendance. Shel is there, sitting beside Sash. Jun fidgets with her papers as Clark drones on. She's worked on this for weeks so it better go well. Then she feels it, low, a vibration within her cunt. The egg.

Jun shifts, uncomfortable. Glances up at Shel, who's smiling.

Jun smirks. Is that all there is?

Clark babbling on and on and a steady buzz between Jun's legs.

Jun shuffles her papers, her transparency falls to the floor.

The egg is doing its work. She shifts and the egg twirls inside her, shifts again, uneasy. Buzzing faster now, and higher, an urgent hum.

Clark steps down. Jun's turn.

But she drops her papers at the podium, and the transparency is lost. There is a burning inside of her, a whirl that spins her off, her mind can't focus and wet, so wet. Her hand shakes, cannot hold the plastic cup, the water splashes over her coil-bound notes. Jun hands out her report, her only hope, and staggers out the door.

Shel follows behind her. "Nice try," a parting shot.

It's Jun's turn to be enraged. She tails Shel down to her office, pushes her to the wall.

But Shel hands her an envelope, says curtly, "Fuck her and I'll pull it out. In the focus room." She slaps a briefcase to Jun. "Fuck her with this. Instructions in the envelope." And Shel exits.

Jun stands, envelope and briefcase in hand.

Jun opens the envelope, dreading. Sash. The instructions are clear.

A knock on Shel's door and Jun opens it. Sash, the new girl on fifth.

Sash asks, "Shel said you wanted to see me?"

The egg hums inside of Jun, she cannot pull away.

"In . . . in the focus room."

On the way down Sash is chattering. "Wouldn't worry . . . great report . . . speaking in public. . . ."

Jun opens the door to the focus room. A wall-sized mirror to her left. Two-way. Jun knows why Shel has chosen this room.

fuck her to the mirror, spread her and let me see it

Jun places the briefcase on the table. Seduction is not her forte. And Sash seems like a sweet young thing. It wasn't as if Jun hadn't caught Sash glancing at her in the washroom, those stares in the boardroom when Sash thought Jun wasn't looking. But this, this was different.

Jun hangs back, sees Sash's lovely neck, her breasts in that loose silky blouse, the skirt clinging to her ass.

Jun stammers, "You, you have a run in your nylons, at, at the back, they're caught, here, turn around."

Sash's eyebrows arch. "That's it? That's all."

Jun thinks, she's expecting more.

Sash turns, but as Jun's hand begins her journey up, Sash looks back, smiling, "I don't wear underwear, not with nylons."

Jun blushes, and Sash is amused.

Sash turns again and Jun's hands run up her legs, to hips.

"Lean forward," Jun whispers hoarsely. Sash places her palms on the table in front of her.

Jun peels down the nylon but only so far. The tightness in her chest, constricting, the air roaring in her ears. Sash's skirt lifted, and Jun can see her pussy, her scent light, not yet thick with desire. The mirror can see them, Jun knows. Jun knows Shel is watching.

With one swift motion Jun grabs Sash's hips, rams her tongue inside her cunt, sucking blindingly, as Sash yelps in surprise, bucking legs but the nylons have got her. Jun eats and eats, mashing her face into Sash's furrow, no subtleties now, her mouth devours, chin rubbing clit, her nose in those folds, her skin, teeth biting ass, Sash's cry, lower, something akin to a moan, as tongue flashes in and out, Jun's mouth gobbling clit and juice, tongue circles, then bullseye the centre, Sash jerks, almost there, but Jun remembers the envelope, the briefcase, and steps back, gulping the air.

Sash blinks, coming to her senses.

Jun glances at the mirror. *Will she do it?*

"Up on the table," Jun commands, and strides forward. Jun begins tearing off Sash's lovely silk shirt, the nylons, the skirt. Sash shivers, cunt clenched, her entire body chafing for touch. Jun sees. Gently she cups Sash's mound, pushes her onto the table, turning Sash on her hands and knees.

The mirror. Such a sweet ass.

"Do you touch yourself, Sash?" Jun asks.

Sash nods.

"Then fuck yourself for me."

Sash hesitates, "Touch me," she whispers.

Jun slaps her hard, between the legs. Sash jolts against the sting.

But Sash begins. Her position is difficult, and Jun feels for her. Sash's fingers are nimble, the juices coming quick. Jun sees the sweat beading on Sash's back, the arching line of bone and muscle, straining thighs, round ass cheeks, taut belly, and breasts in limbo. Sash is so perfect like this, the mirror catches her, her cunt a revelation.

With a start, Jun sees the video camera in the corner and knows Shel's preserving this.

Sash's staccato gasps, she's so close to coming, but Jun takes her hand away.

"Please, Jun." Sash looks so desperate now.

Jun eases her off the table. "Catch your breath."

Jun goes to the briefcase, snaps it open. Inside, a harness and dildo. A bow and ribbon, reading *For Sash*.

Jun strips off her clothes, straps on the harness and dildo. Sash watches. Her chest is flushed, glossy.

"Jun," she says, "I've never . . . not with that."

Jun guides her to the table, lifts her up. "Not if you don't want to," Jun murmurs. And at last begins tasting those nipples, grasping breasts she presses them together, takes both of those small buds into her mouth. Sash moans, feels the sucking down to her cunt. Jun revels in the fullness in her hands, the play of pebbles in her mouth, she feels Sash wanting her, makes her want to fuck her more.

Jun nudges Sash back on the table, pushes open Sash's thighs, matted curls, a dark flush within, the liquid seeping out of her cunt hole, viscous.

"Eat me," Sash begs.

Jun only smiles. She nestles the tip of her dildo at the edge of Sash's lips, the barest hint of motion.

"Sash," Jun whispers. The dildo brushes. "Sash." The dildo's caress.

"Jun, I've never. . . ."

Jun looks down at her, rocks a smidgen in. Sash feels it, and Jun rocks out.

"One word," Jun murmurs, "and I'm out of here." A promise or a threat? Rocks deeper, but only slightly. Rocks and rocks, no deeper, but Sash can feel it, and instinctively tries to pull the dildo in as it pulls away.

Rocks. Rocks. No more, no less.

Sash has to ask, to beg.

Rocks.

"Deeper, please."

Jun complies, but barely. Sash's hips are up, but Jun forces her down.

"Deeper, Jun, please."

Again.

Sash, in tears, cannot hold back, "Oh, fuck me."

Jun does just that, plowing into her, and fuck slam fuck of rutting joy, reaming bliss, a humping, bucking animalistic greed, not for the camera, not for Shel, but her her her, a piercing, cleansing need. The egg spins inside of her, like she's fucking herself, and Shel behind the mirror, she can see all of this.

Jun pulls out. Sash is on the table, barely able to move, yet she's still not come. Jun's mouth suckles Sash's slit, her fingers thrust into her cunt, she pumps and swallows, pumps and swallows, Sash's leg over Jun's shoulder, hips jerking at each penetration, Jun's mouth latching onto Sash's clit, sucking, fingers fucking as Sash's swept into her coming.

♀

The room goes dark and the door opens. At first Jun does not believe it, a cake with candles, Shel, and Olivia from fifth floor singing "Happy Birthday" to Sash. Sash, still on the table, legs open, feels the whipping cream on her clit, just as Olivia licks it off.

"Happy birthday, girl," Olivia laughs.

Jun blinks in surprise.

Shel links arms with Olivia, partners in crime.

Olivia pushes back Sash's disheveled hair, her hand slinking down into Sash's vagina. "Oh, I'm going to have a fun time tonight," Olivia whispers, "watching Jun fuck you, and with my birthday gift too. What a birthday wish, are you surprised it came true?"

Jun, the egg still planted inside her, looks at Shel, asking.

Shel glances at her watch, shakes her head. "Eleven o'clock and we've only started."

First

The first night had been simple. A drink, a dance, some witty conversation, hints about old lovers. An open door, a kiss, and you can still remember the sight of her cunt, that dewy invitation. All the next day you can smell that heady perfume on your fingers, savour the salty lingerings in your mouth. Simple.

The second night became the third, the generous spread of lips, her tongue nibbling across your nipples, her breasts crushed along your back, the ride of her mound as she rubbed thigh, smearing wetness, your bucking pride as she slid into your ass.

The fourth night you fucked her outside, at the fence behind the bar, arms spread, legs wide, pumped her to the beat of the music, her knees gave way but you didn't care, one arm carried her as the other fucked her into the air.

Fifth night she slammed into you from behind, packing eight inches and that was a surprise, arriving early, and you, just from the shower, bending over to see the present she had dropped. Fifth night you moaned and still she would not let you go, pushing through, pushing through, the keening pulse of your need, churning inside. Fifth night and she doesn't let you touch her, she fucks and she fucks, takes you always from behind, takes you like you want her, fucking you alive.

Sixth night and you've been walking funny all day. She comes

Night

into your apartment and you look for the tormenting bulge, but it's not there. Sixth night, she strips you, presses cold towels to ease the itch, an ice cube for the swelling. Sixth night she only watches as ice cube after ice cube melts between your legs. Sixth night is wet but chilling as she spreads your butt cheeks, opens your thighs, ice along your clitoris, the shaft and tender hood, ice stroking lips and lips, ice pushed deep inside. Sixth night and you want her hands, her fingers, her mouth, you even want the cock back. But sixth night and she shakes her head, saying you're too sore.

Seventh night you take her to the cottage by the lake, then down to the end of the docks. You notice her skirt, no bulge, but you're packing yourself and you can feel the tightness in your crotch. Seventh night and you've learned never to assume. On the dock, you rip off her skirt and explore her pussy. She hasn't let you touch her for days and her cunt looks almost virginal. But you, you've been tricked and goaded, teased into a hunger that stabs you to the core. You push her down on her stomach, bunch up your jacket and slide it under her hips. Seventh night and her cunt is raised, an offering, you undo your zipper and free your cock into the warm air, you haven't kissed her, licked her, but she's glistening and for a moment you stare. You stare.

Sweet pussy. Beauty's haven. A scent of heaven.

She calls your name, thighs shaking, and you stroke her ass cheeks as they slap against your hips. Seventh night and you fuck her long and hard, but never enough to come, always pulling out just before her time, slowing the rhythm, or the angle, or the rhyme. She's crying, hips jerking, knees rising, but you push her down, and you ask if she's enjoying the ride. You pull out and a sob's dragged out of her, blood rush building.

You take out another cock, clamp it on, a screw–ridged silicone that vibrates and gyrates, three speeds and brand–spanking–new batteries. She hears the buzz and turns, cannot see it, your knees knocking her thighs wider, your hands grab her hips and you sit back, let her have the illusion of control, ease her onto your whirling humming, she doesn't know what's coming but she feels it, this new sensation, her joy, she moves to her rhythm, bearing down on your gift, this rapture, don't need to fuck her, she's doing it, doing it, her wetness spilling out of her, splashing you, to the waters below, fuck fuck fuck, she keening, coming desperate now, so hard you've fallen back, she doesn't care, straddles you, all muscle and frenzy and comes, comes down so hard on you, comes slamming hard. Quiet. The lake so quiet. Her panting. She looks so beautiful on top of you. Tenderly, you stroke her back, but it's been a trap all along. Click and the silicone ripples higher, speeding faster, a look of confusion as she's thrown, a thrust of your hips so hard she stumbles, but she can't get the silicone out of her in time, a forward lurch and you're still inside, climbing, thrusting, rutting inside. Tears now, she's all thrashing need, she comes, fists smacking the dock planks as her spasms subside.

The loons on the lake cry back to you.

But you don't let this hold her, another click and full speed now, your cock spinning inside, her screaming rage and you don't let her go, you fuck and fuck and fuck, each orgasm peaking her, or tearing her apart, it takes longer, much longer to push her to that edge and she's begging you harder, this movement, her body contracting, begging to be fucked hard. The sun's coming up and the batteries are dying, but still you fuck her, fill her, until one last thrust, sinking in, you sleep.

Seventh day and you wake on the dock. She dozes, beneath you, your cock firmly inside. You ease out of her and she wakes, muscles clutching at the loss. You promise her a breakfast of waffles and pancakes, but you know she's going to be eating you out. Stealthily you smooth what's left of the lube onto the silicone. Come, you'll carry her, you say, arms around her hips, legs around your waist. And she does this willingly, though barely awake.

Your finger slides.

Her eyes snap open.

Yes, you ask.

Again, she whispers.

A shift and you lift her, a hesitation before you enter, but you do, a cry pushed out of her, then a whimper and a shiver, and with every stride you fuck her, every bounce, every step, you carry her cunt on your cock, down the dock, up the path, to the cottage below.

Love

Jen checks herself into the Love Hotel, apprehensive and skittish. It doesn't look like a hotel, just a big Victorian with creeping vines and a solid middle class veneer. Jen plays with the red plastic tag attached to her key. She is having second thoughts.

A neutral space, her therapist had recommended, for Jen and the sex surrogate. A woman.

But I'm straight, Jen had protested.

All the better, the therapist had replied, for emotional distance. Besides, I know just the person for you.

So Jen sits on the edge of the bed at the Love Hotel, her night bag at her feet. She wants to jump out the window when there is a knock at the door.

Come in.

Chris walks in and Jen is baffled. Chris is a thirty–something woman, wearing a suit and tie. She carries a black leather briefcase and looks like the young urban professional she is.

Hi.

Hello. Jen is taken aback.

They shake hands.

Jen notices Chris's hands, fine and tapered fingers, soft and strong.

Chris smiles. Doctor's Glaster's referral? she asks.

Hotel

Yes, I'm –

But Chris cuts in. No names.

Jen shakes her head, not quite understanding.

But Chris has already turned around and opened her briefcase.

She places the case in front of Jen.

In the case, lubricant, four differently-shaped dildos, various body straps and harnesses, three vibrators, a velvet glove, latex and lube, a loop of condoms, and some other devices Jen has never even imagined.

Jen steps back.

Don't worry, Chris assures her, you're in control here. These are just . . . possibilities. Shall we begin? Without waiting for an answer Chris strips off her clothes, revealing her hidden assets, soft breasts, the curves of hips and thighs. Chris slips into the bed and turns to Jen.

Jen gasps, But I'm straight.

Chris looks at her, explaining, This isn't about who you fuck, it's about how you feel.

Jen looks to the door. Chris follows the look, waits for her decision and says gently, It's all right, it's your choice, no rush.

And for Jen, the gentleness clinches it. She slips off her dress, her bra and panties, slips into the sheets, if a bit stiffly, but still. . . .

Chris curls around her, feels the tremors of fear, the fluttering indecisions. Breathe, she whispers.

Jen shakes out her breath and Chris smiles. Jen looks at her and laughs. Ridiculous, really. She looks at Chris, looks at her for the first time, and sees the sardonic smile and the arch of her eyebrow.

Why do you do this? Jen asks.

I'm good at it.

Jen looks at the briefcase and Chris answers, Not tonight. Tonight is just touch.

And so they begin.

Chris strokes Jen's back, as Jen finds a need to explain: her boyfriend, this fear, her need for a surrogate. Chris listens, no judgments, as her hands caress beneath the sheets. Jen blushes. Chris's touch is tender, and if Jen could describe it, protective. Jen feels her wetness, the slippery slope of her moral confusion. She feels the fullness of her chest, the tightness of her belly. Her cunt is slick and her breasts tingle at the lightness of stroke. She is dizzy with possibilities and with apprehensions. All this, Chris seems to know.

Chris pulls off the sheet.

Jen snaps her legs shut. Fear flutters in her throat, tears in her eyes.

It's all right, Chris soothes. But it's important for you to see this. Do you want to touch me?

Jen blinks. This is unexpected. Chris reads this in her eyes.

You always want to please. Make love to me like you want to be loved, and then we'll see what I can do for you.

This, Jen understands, her need to please others. And Chris waits. Jen reaches out. Her touch is timid, inadvertently teasing against Chris's skin. Be greedy, Chris whispers, a hoarseness creeping into her voice. Jen hears the need in Chris's demand, the undertone of desire. She rocks back, astonished. And why? Because she is a woman? Jen chokes back her surprise, glances at the door. She feels as if she is drowning, the tide pulling her from shore.

Chris waits, confident and assured. Twenty-two, she guesses, or twenty-five and still Jen's never come, not with her boyfriend, not with anyone. But she has journeyed this far, still trembling, the uncertainty clear in her eyes. Chris softens, tries to remember her own fumbling beginnings, how the body knows, but the mind cowers, afraid and wretchedly ashamed. Does she know what she is capable of? Pleasure is such a simple thing.

Chris smiles and opens her thighs. Jen stares and stares. She has never seen another woman's vagina, not like this, this giving, naked sexuality. Jen looks into Chris's eyes, her chest flooding with sudden tears. She swallows them, bewildered. Chris's eyes are kind as she pulls her down. Hesitant, Jen kisses her lips, stinging kisses as Chris rubs against her. Jen feels her own power, as she retreats, realizing, *she wants me.* She stares at Chris, at her nakedness, her open passion. Her lips fall to Chris's breast, her hands cupping, her tongue playing with nipples as they swell in her mouth, sucking, tongue swirling over and over, she has never touched a woman's breasts, soft, a yielding fullness. Jen's fingers, tentative, trace down to Chris's belly, the strong, wiry hairs, how crisp they feel, and so warm, a different heat as she brushes deeper, how the moistness rises, glistens. Chris gasps and now Jen wants to fuck her, this pleasure in giving pleasure as Jen's fingers slip into Chris, deep into her, this newness, warm and slick, it shocks her and Jen slips down, watching her fingers go into Chris, Chris pulling her in, cunt muscles clutching at her, building this rhythm. Chris moans her need and the sound pulls Jen out of her.

Jen stares at Chris, a sheen of sweat across her chest, her breasts gleaming with Jen's saliva.

Chris blink, blinks, breathless. Her cunt is empty. Aching.

I'm sorry. Jen is close to tears. I don't think I can do this.

Chris sighs, ragged. She bites her lip, bites down on her frustration. Her breasts pinch and her cunt is throbbing. She curls herself up and Jen can see her wetness, how she has wet the sheets. She has teased her into this, Jen can see the red, swollen vaginal lips, the sticky pubic curls. Chris cups her hand over her pussy. Jen sees the shaking hand, feels how close she has come without coming. Chris closes her eyes, breathes deeply. It's all right.

But Jen can hear the disappointment hidden in her voice.

Chris reaches over to the briefcase, takes out a long slender vibrator. She looks over to Jen, explaining, I've got to. . . . Chris looks the tiniest bit sheepish. Could you . . . hold me while I come? Jen nods. Chris lies back, turns on the vibrator. She pauses a moment, then asks, Do you want to hold it? Surprised, Jen holds the buzzing toy in her hand. Chris opens her legs. Carefully Jen places it against Chris's mons, and gently begins stroking her lips. Chris is humming, her eyes hooded, languor seeping into her limbs. Jen stares, spreads Chris wider. She goes in close, listening for the catches in Chris's breath, the movement of hips. She stares at her, dark glistening, hears the slightest whimper, the twitch of thigh. The vibrator hums. Sticky wet. Jen wonders how Chris tastes, salty or sweet. Jen thinks of her fingers, the strong grip of cunt muscles pulling her in. She raises the head of the vibrator, teases it between Chris's lips and feels Chris shaking beneath her, quickening. Stroke and stroke again, in, out, how those cunt lips can take this in, Chris's whimpers keening into moans, Jen can smell her, this close, this rich heavy scent, wetness covering the shaft of the vibrator, she pulls it out, as Chris bucks in protest.

Chris sits up, blinks. What?

Jen shakes the vibrator. It's not buzzing.

Chris bites down, crosses over the bed on her knees, looks into the briefcase.

Jen sits, behind her. She can see Chris's pussy, slick and dripping. She has never been this close, never tasted, never thought of . . . . but she stares at Chris's round ass and her hands grab her softness, her tongue glides into her, she can smell her musky perfume, taste the salty juice, her tongue flicking deeper,

Chris's deep and shuddering groan, the shock of Jen *there*, her cunt on fire, arms giving way, tongue thrusting, fucking her, but Jen pulls her back, flips her over. She wants to see and taste and feel. She falls on Chris's pussy, sucking on her clit, and Chris, her hand in Jen's hair she can't hold back and Jen's fingers sliding in pushing her up –

Jen slides out and Chris is left hanging again. This tempo is maddening. Jen looks to the briefcase, asks, Can I do it with those?

Chris nods, the burn in her cunt blotting out all of Glaster's prescriptions. She watches as Jen fumbles with the harness straps, can't quite do up the straps. Chris helps her, but her fingers are trembling, she needs it long and hard now, but Jen, her first time, her uncertainties, that crippling icy fear. . . .

Chris takes a breath, sighs as Jen guides the shaft, so close, god, so slowly in. Her knees are weak, her arms, they shake and the twitch in her cunt is torturing. Jen, on top of her, doesn't want to hurt, but this rhythm is not fast enough, her gentleness a sting –

"Fuck me like a woman," Chris commands, and Jen pauses, if only for a moment, stares into Chris's eyes, at her permission to let it all go. Jen, who knows that sex is not simple, sometimes not even kind, starts at this revelation. Jen knows Chris wants her, wants this badly. And me? Jen wonders. Jen stares at the sinews in Chris's throat, feels the gentle nudge she gives contract Chris's body whole. And she knows. Jen wants to fuck her like she's never been taken, fuck her to a place she's never been to before. She plunges into Chris's cunt, throbbing, thrusting, her hips going wild, she's fucking her for every woman she's ever desired, every kiss she's never known, slamming into her with all her empty nights, those silent longings, the hum in her blood, her singing bones, Jen fucks her like she means it, fucks her till she's sore. Jen fucks long into the night, into this movement she wants to call home.

Hot

Suzanne steps but does not sink into the smooth drift of snow. The snowshoes are cumbersome but they do the trick. Behind her, Mika struggles. They have come this far and the hot spring is close by, the sky glowing and snowflakes wafting down. The trees, in their starkness, are especially striking, their icy branches extending above them, crackling, crackling against the blue. Suzanne looks behind her, sees Mika shift and stumble. Suzanne laughs because is it a beautiful day and all is right with the world.

Mika is not so sure. All night she has lain awake, listening to the sounds of her friend Jessie and Suzanne thrashing in their bedroom. Her best friend Jessie. This retreat was supposed to be a buddies outing, but here she is, Suzanne, tagging along. And now this. Mika had wanted to explore the hot spring alone, after this morning, but Jessie had been worried, the threat of cougars, bears, avalanches. Mika groused, As if, but Jessie had won, as she always did. Besides, Jessie added, you and Suzanne should get to know each other.

Look, Suzanne points. The hot spring.

Mika glances up, irritated. Suzanne, who always got everything first.

The cave is low and deep, barely visible through the thick mist that hovers in the air. Suzanne and Mika scramble into the

Spring

entrance. They can see the smooth rock, the twists and grooves formed by the water trickling, the ever present steam, stalactites and stalagmites, worn from the walls, the ceiling, the floor.

They strip off their clothes and step into this strange, subterranean world. Oddly enough, it is not too dark. The mouth of the cave reflects the glow of the outside snow, the walls gleam and their eyes adjust to the dimness. They slip into the spring. Hot, very hot, the slippery rock.

Mika sits back, her body steeping in this warmth, her worries bubble through her skin, dissipate into the air.

Hot, hot. The waters, still. And then, a movement.

Mika sees Suzanne rising from the pool, skin flushed from the heat. Suzanne walks to her backpack and fetches her thermos. She drinks from the cap, then gestures, offering. Mika shakes her head. Suzanne sits at the edge of the pool, dipping her legs into the pool, basking in the steam.

Mika closes her eyes. When she opens them she sees Suzanne, legs still dangling, but she has lain back on the rock, her thighs parted, her cunt, so like a cave, the ripples and folds.

Mika closes her eyes again. But beating, on the backs of her eyelids, the vision of this morning. She had come back from a solitary walk and stood by the window of the cottage. Glancing

in she had seen them. She had watched. Jessie in the overstuffed
chair, naked, legs pulled open, draped over the arms of the chair,
Suzanne between them, eating her out. Jessie, her face so intent,
so concentrated, the waves of pleasure rocking her hair down,
over her eyes, her hands on Suzanne's head, she was so close, so
close that Mika could imagine fucking her, her own hand in those
plummeting depths. Her head thrown back, Jessie had looked up,
looked at her at the window, as Suzanne fucked away, her mouth
feeling the pull of Jessie's cunt. Jessie, staring at Mika staring at her,
the sight so raw and keening, Jessie coming, Mika hearing her cries
through the window, in the quiet of the woods.

Suzanne's face, in Jessie's cunt, but Mika had seen it, the look
in Jessie's eyes.

Mika stands, dizzy. Too hot. She gets up from the pool and
lies down on the smooth rock floor. She turns on her stomach,
the heat shimmering from her body. Cool stone, the air, a floating
embrace. She dozes.

Mika stirs, feels a touch, this surprise, beginning along the
back of her calves, then into that sensitive dip behind her knees, a
trace up her thigh. Suzanne eases herself down, presses her breasts
into Mika's ass, her mouth into the small of her back, a gentle
rub against her, and Mika's legs part, Suzanne's hands on Mika's
waist.

Mika turns, sliding Suzanne off, I can't, I can't do this to her.
To Jessie.

They dress in silence, awkward. The trek back to the cottage is
excruciatingly long.

Suzanne goes directly into the bedroom, to Jessie, closes the
door. Low whispers. The cottage, quiet. It is getting dark. Mika
tiptoes into the kitchen. She can hear the muffled conversation,
can't make out the words, but she knows that this is serious. The
air feels brooding, heavy. She doesn't like this. She doesn't like this
one bit.

Jessie comes out, lights the candles in the living room, her manner contemplative. For Mika, it is becoming unbearable.

Jessie – she begins, but stops. What can she say?

Jessie turns, leans into her with a long, heartfelt kiss. A kiss, deep and exploring, a shiver shuddering into Mika's centre, Jessie's hands cupping her breasts, Mika's shock spiraling into wonder. Mika's belt is unbuckled, pants yanked down and a mouth pushes into her pussy, Suzanne behind her, a jolting realization. A flutter in her belly, but as Suzanne licks, Mika's senses sink into her cunt, her struggles swamped by her need. Mika is spread and swallowed, sucked and stroked, two mouths devouring both lips, she can barely stand. Jessie breaks away, gazes as Suzanne takes Mika, pushes her against the chair, eats her slowly, wants this to last, Jessie watching, this heaving motion, a smile, this feast for the eyes.

Jessie sits on the couch, pulls off her jeans and begins touching herself, on display. Mika cannot take her eyes off her, even as she's being taken, Jessie, fucking herself, for her.

Mika is almost there, the movement between her legs spiraling out of control.

But Suzanne stops, smiles, strips off the shirt, her jeans, tosses the panties. She lies down in front of Mika, spreads herself on the floor. Mika can see her, see the folds, the budding clitoris, the wetness of her vagina.

Mika, Suzanne whispers. Suzanne's eyes are dark, veiled by the weight of her longing. Mika looks into Suzanne's openness, remembers the steaming hot spring, the rosy cave, but she hesitates, uncertain, glances at Jessie.

Jessie smiles.

And Mika smiles back. She kneels down between Suzanne legs. Her hands on either side of Suzanne's thighs, her thumbs on that bushy mound, she pushes up, so slightly, the hood over clit retracting. Fingers lower now, Mika parts Suzanne's labia, to the slickness below. Is this what Jessie sees, glistening heat, this offering. Mika opens the inner lips, to the secrets held there, and slides her tongue into that hot slickness, feels the contraction of Suzanne's inner walls, her whimper that cuts through air.

Suzanne is so warm, so sweet, this aroma. Mika slips into her, tightness expanding, beating into a rhythm and she has to ride. Mika pushes her into her cries, rocking hips, and she cannot hold. So close and Mika can feel it in the crush of her knuckles. Suzanne comes, squeezing Mika's fingers out of her, but Mika presses on, pushes wave after wave.

Mika rests, places her head on Suzanne's belly, feels her hand stroking through her hair.

Thank you, Suzanne murmurs. I've wanted you for such a long time.

Jessie watches.

The air, stifling, too hot, too close.

Mika rises, fast. She is dizzy, the room spinning out of control. So that's what this is, she accuses, a gift for your girlfriend.

Is that what you think?

Mika pushes Jessie to the chair, surprised at her own reaction, this swift, sudden play. She pushes out those legs, and sinks into her pussy. No frills, no foreplay, it's all cunt, cunt, cunt, as Mika fucks her with a raw, naked passion. Mika, no longer at the window, but here making Jessie beg, making Jessie plead, tasting and smelling and touching, more than she can imagine, Mika fucking Jessie like it was years before.

Suzanne stares at Mika, sweet shining ass, her cozy pussy. She can see wetness, how Mika's body undulates as she eats Jessie out. Legs spreading as she goes deeper, but Suzanne can see, see the droplets glistening on her mound, how her cunt pushes out the lower Mika goes, how naked she is, how enticingly exposed.

Suzanne's fingers dive in. Mika bucks, feels the fullness. She resists, squirming, as if to elude those fingers, to push them out, but Suzanne only plunges deeper and Mika can feel her cunt blooming. Mika groans. She doesn't want it like this, wants it to be Jessie but her body holds, fiercely clutching those fingers, sucking her in as Suzanne draws her out. A string of stinging bites along her shoulders, and Mika's thrown, as Jessie slides down and begins kissing Mika's breasts, Jessie feasting, teasing, laughing at Mika's surprise. Jessie smiles as her hand snakes down, stroking Mika's clit as Suzanne's hand fucks Mika's slick and streaming cunt. Mika comes, fucked and stroked, her body out of control, whose hands, whose fingers, she no longer knows.

♀

Later, when Mika wakes, she will wonder. Suzanne, loosed–limbed and languid, lies beside her. Jessie's leg, thrown over Mika hips, a proprietary gesture, even in sleep. But for once, and perhaps forever, it is Suzanne who Mika sees, Suzanne who dreams and asks, so simply, as if desire were not an improbable, impossible joy. And for this night, who gives and who takes, in this morning with the light glistening over the lip of the window pane, this glow shimmering across such fragile trembling flesh, Suzanne, Mika, and Jessie, all together and all alone.

Sachi remembered the first time it had come up. Aimi, giving her a slow finger fuck, asking about fantasies, had teased it out of her. But she put it away from her mind. Besides, there were some things about herself she preferred not to know.

Tonight, after the two pots of tea that Aimi claimed was an aphrodisiac, Aimi had said, Touch yourself for me. So Sachi began, a bit self-consciously, sliding her fingers down onto her mound, began stroking, not on her clit but above it. The fleshy hood rubbed over and over the tiny tender button.

Aimi, licking her lips, stared at the wetness bubbling up and over.

Don't come, Aimi said. Not yet. Aimi slid her face between Sachi's legs, staring, kissed, not her clit, not her vagina, but the space between, sucking at the tiny hole, the urethra.

Aimi, Sachi realized, knees shaking, I've got to pee.

Aimi smiled.

Aimi took Sachi's foot, placed it between her legs and began to move, smearing her juices as she rocked. Surprised, Sachi gasped, but Aimi leaned back and slid Sachi's toe into her cunt. Sachi stared. Her toe in that delicate pussy, such a touch and Aimi could be so open.

But Aimi didn't let it last. She reached forward and lifted Sachi's

Rain

foot from her cunt. She smelled herself, licked off her own juices and as she sucked and nibbled, Aimi saw Sachi's cunt squirm.

She smiled as Sachi gaped. You are such a prude.

Sachi blushed. She stood.

Where are you going?

To the can.

Sachi walked away. She had to go really badly, that tea went right through her. But Aimi was behind, guiding her into the shower stall.

What –

Hold it, Aimi said. Hold it for as long as you can. And kneeling, she pushed Sachi against the wall and began sucking.

Sachi blinked. Her cunt was so swollen, and Aimi's tongue so deft, but the pressure on her bladder was becoming painful, incessant.

Aimi sucked on her clit, wouldn't let her go.

Aimi, Sachi pleaded, but for what she didn't quite know. She shifted her legs, angling for some kind of relief, but movement only made the feeling worse. She clenched her cunt muscles, but Aimi's tongue slid, tickling her out. She thought she would burst but she held it in, held on, tormented by her bladder bearing down and Aimi's strokes on her clit.

Aimi, Sachi begged, I can't hold it, I can't. . . .

Aimi sat back, brushed up Sachi's pubic hair. Her thumbs skirted along the edge of her lips, parted them further. Sachi's clit was swollen, engorged, just a few more flicks would send her over the edge. But Aimi slid her fingers into her cunt, stroked the vaginal wall towards Sachi's bladder.

Sachi squirted, felt a sudden burning shame but she clenched, desperately trying to hold it in. Her hips were shaking, Aimi's hands holding her up, Aimi sucking so fiercely, Aimi inside her, unraveling all of her restraints, so close to coming, she couldn't hold back.

A last gasp for control, but Aimi, fingers fucking, pushed her over.

Sachi cried out.

She came, a flooding surge, such blessed relief, pissing on Aimi's breasts, showering her, a jerking stream through her contractions, splashing her warmth over Aimi's stomach, Aimi's thighs as Aimi gaped at her gushing prize, that little hole letting loose, letting go. Aimi leaned into Sachi's spray as Sachi gazed at her, as the yellow liquid cascaded down. Sachi, emptied, this protracted release, this pressure easing, swept into a shuddering surrender.

Sachi slid down, crumbled to her knees.

Aimi held her, swept back her tumbling hair. See, that wasn't so bad. No thunderbolts, no lightning. See? You don't have to be afraid of your fantasies.

The

Lisa sat in the kitchen. Eight o'clock and still no sign of Sera. She sighed, glanced over the table to the rice congealed in the bowl, the soggy tonkatsu on the plate. Another Saturday night.

There was a turn in the latch and Sera stood in the doorway.

"Sorry I'm late," she murmured, her brace hitting the hall table as she closed the door. Sera always worked late. At least since the accident.

"Do you want some —"

"No, I've already eaten."

Sera shuffled to the washroom, popped her pills for the pain, brushed her teeth. She sank into the bed, back towards Lisa.

"Long day?"

"Long day." And Sera clicked off the light.

♀

Morning and Lisa woke, the space beside her empty. She rose, made her way to the kitchen, to Sera sitting at the table, coffee in hand.

"You're up early."

Sera turned to the paper. "I have work to do."

"How about if we go back to bed . . . put on some music. . . ."

Sera picked up the video on the table. "What's this?" And read

Accident

from the package, "The All–Night Pussy Party."

Lisa blushed. "Leila lent it to me. I . . . I thought we could watch it . . . it's just that we haven't. . . ."

Their eyes locked.

Sera stood, grabbed the brace in her hand. "Well, have fun." And she limped out of the room.

Lisa was right behind her. "If you want to go back to him, go back to him. Just make up your mind and let me get on with my life."

"Is that what this is about?"

Lisa was on the brink, but she no longer cared. "You slink out every time I come into the room. Obviously you haven't gotten him out of your fucking system, so make up your goddamn mind!"

Lisa stormed back into the bedroom, began packing her bags. Sera watched from the doorway.

"I made a mistake," Sera said simply.

"Mistakes? You don't make mistakes. I could understand if you were the kind of person who thought with their cunt, but no, you don't even look at me anymore." Lisa took a ragged breath, pulled herself together. "Besides, it's over."

Sera sat on the bed. "You haven't given me much time –"

"Given *you* much time?"

"– and you haven't forgiven me."

"Damn right I haven't forgiven you!" Lisa shouted.

"What would be the point, then?"

Lisa and Sera. What would be the point.

♀

The next day Lisa came by to drop off the key. She rang the doorbell. "Christ, let's not make this any harder."

No answer.

Grumbling, she let herself in.

Lisa kicked off her shoes, flung her coat on the chair, and marched into the kitchen.

Sera was waiting.

"Didn't you hear –"

"Do you realize," Sera began calmly, "every time we've made love, I've always fucked you first. I've always initiated and then fucked you. Now why is that?"

"This isn't the time –" Lisa started slipping past but Sera pushed her back.

"Did you think I was too tired, or too crabby? Why didn't you make the effort? Maybe I just wanted you to reach for me, for once in your life."

Lisa looked at Sera.

"I'm not the one chasing dick."

"At least he wanted me."

"And I don't?"

"Do you, Lisa? You weren't paying much attention until he came along."

Lisa looked away.

Sera placed her hand on Lisa's belly, slid inside her pants.

"Are you wet for me, Lisa, or is it just habit?" and Sera kissed her, long and lingering. Lisa's hand, running through Sera's hair, familiar as well.

Sera pulled away. "At least you're wet now." Sera stood. "Tell me, did it get too boring, the same position, fuck after fuck. We could have. . . ." Sera pushed away. Tears. Tears in Sera's eyes.

Lisa has never seen this before. "It's not my fault."

"I know, Lisa. But it's not all mine either."

Lisa held her, took her hand. Cold. Sera was cold.

"Come on." Lisa led her out of the room. "I know just what you need."

♀

Lisa adjusted the temperature of the shower, hot, steaming hot, the way Sera liked it. The shower had support bars, and a small plastic seat bolted to the wall, just in case.

Sera could cry in the shower, the one place she had learned to let go.

Water, soothing, droplets of spray, caressing, hiding the tears. Lisa began soaping Sera's back as she held her. Her formidable lover, always so sure, so strong. Lisa sighed. In her arms, she felt so much smaller. Stupid, stupid, how could Lisa not have seen it?

They swayed, a slow dance in the shower.

"I'm sorry," Sera whispered.

"I know."

"I said it was an accident but . . . I shouldn't have slept with him."

"I know."

They danced.

"I love you."

Lisa smiled. "I know."

Sera pulled back, squinted against the steam. "Sometimes you are just so –"

Lisa laughed, deep in her belly. Sighed. "Why couldn't we do this before?"

"Because I felt guilty. Because you were mad at me."

Lisa stroked her cheek. "Damn it, even when you lose, it's like you win." Sera's face, tiny wrinkles around her eyes. Ten years, and they both deserved better from each other.

Lisa pressed Sera against the seat, cupped Sera's breasts in her hands. "How could you possibly think that I didn't desire you?" Lisa kissed her familiar mouth, but she was always so new, always surprising her. Had she ever told her? Breasts, Lisa loved those breasts, loved sucking out her nipples, loved stroking out her moans. Sera always came like she was fighting it, grasping at every shred of self-control. Lisa smiled, slid down the curve of belly, and she brushed back those curls, to hooded clitoris and wavy lips, a kiss so slow that Sera began to shake, but Lisa was holding her, tongue snaking, slithering into grooves, tangy sweetness of her, Lisa sucking and stroking, not letting her go.

♀

On the bed, with Sera's head on her belly, Lisa, falling back into the calm of the room.

"We could get one of those sex swings," she said, "You know, or check out those catalogues, vibrators and . . . do-hickies." But Lisa couldn't help it, she was already blushing.

"Do-hickies?" Sera laughed. "Oh, you are an innocent at heart."

"Well, you know. For when we hit the next rough patch."

"Sex is not going to solve everything." Sera's lips on her belly, her fingers dancing below.

"I've missed you."

Sera's lips, stroking lower, a kiss that sends shivers through Lisa's cunt.

"I've missed you too."

Too many drinks in too many bars and she just wants one good fuck. Damn that Jeanie. She leans against the cold rail and that clears her mind. She can walk, anyway. Then in the elevator of her apartment building she spots him.

Young, but not too young, handsome but not a muscle man, leather jacket and torn jeans and a nice friendly smile.

She smiles back, realizes she's seen him before.

She stumbles and he catches her, holds her arm. A gentleman.

God, she wants to fuck him.

An invitation to her apartment. He's quiet, though. She kisses him and places his hand on her breast.

It's inside her door that she tells him. Not without a condom.

He steps back, rocks on his heels.

She finds a condom in the pocket of her purse, tugs on his leather jacket, leads him to the bed. She strips, fast, she wants this so bad.

He is quiet.

Shy, she thinks, and laughs at the thought of seducing him.

She spreads her legs. Fuck me.

He can see her, see how wet she is for him.

Turn around, he whispers, staring.

Jeanie

She turns, on her hands and knees, and feels his hands on her ass, his kisses, his tongue. His fingers part her slit and she rocks as he works his tongue deeper.

A gentleman.

Fuck me, she wails, but he takes his time.

She hears the tear of plastic wrap.

Don't turn around, he whispers.

But she feels it, the tip, skirting the outside of her cunt, and she pushes down to reach it, but he pulls away.

His hands grab her hips as she's wiggling her ass, eases it in slowly so she can feel every inch, a vicious jab at the end, pulling out.

She gasps. He's playing rough now.

In again. He feels so different, so hard. She tells herself it is the condom, this angle, she's never done it like this before.

He grunts, as he plows into her, so hard he lifts up her knees. Nothing gentle about it.

Faster now, his breath blowing, he hasn't taken off any of his clothes, but she's so naked, opening, thrust by thrust.

She likes this, wants it badly and she goads him with her cries.

He pulls her to the edge of the bed, thrusting wilder, so hard he's ramming her, she's coming, coming, crying out begging, fucks so fiercely she feels him plunging into the deepest part of her, ripping her apart but she's taking it, this movement, her cunt coming, she can't hold, crying, cursing, stomach lifted off the bed, spasms riding bucking hips slapped down, fucking cunt clenching she comes, like rolling thunder, electric spasms, twitching, holding him in.

She rests, panting. Sweat beading on her back.

He's still hard inside of her. Moves so slowly. Begins again.

She can't believe it, hasn't even begun to recover, but so easily aroused, her body responding, a low and snarling groan, hips tilted ever so slightly to take him, not that he's even sliding out, how easily he stokes her, nudges, coaxes the juices out, she can even hear her wetness, the sticky slurp of dick moving in and out, but he starts, short staccato thrusts as she begins her keening moans, takes her faster to the edge, growling if she can take it, he fucks her deeper, stabbing, moves his hips a different motion, so hard, still so hard, how could he still be so hard, she's coming, wants it faster, too much, too much, she'll feel him days later, pain skirting the edge of pleasure, she wants him to come inside her, feel him wither in her cunt, tries to hold out but she tumbles, muscles rippling, hands slapping the bed, fast, an orgasm so deep it's no longer a release but a sobbing fucked-out need.

He's still inside her. Hard.

He slides out. Sees the pussy lips, swollen. He's churned her, cunt bubbles, frothing.

She turns. See him, lying back. His dick. His rubber dick.

She rises, cunt aching, falls, slapping, arms flailing, falls against him, feels breasts, the binding through the denim shirt, the slightness of frame. He turns her, pulls her off, pins her down, her grunts, spitting fury, but his mouth on her breasts, as he thrusts, grinding her into the floor.

He fucks her so mindless and rutting, this fuck-bursting, cunt-pumping joy, this movement as she opens and opens, jumble of sweat smell and wetjuice, this calling, the only god she's ever known.

♀

When she wakes, she sees her, examining her swollen cunt.

Jeanie, she scolds, that was a bit too much.

Jeanie leans forward, looks at the woman's pussy. Contrite, she asks, I didn't hurt you, did I? Jeanie licks her clit, as the other woman wriggles. Pushed away, Jeanie looks up but she can see her cunt is swimming. Jeanie knows she likes it hard.

The woman picks up the harness and straps it on. Smiles. She knows Jeanie's bluffs and blusters, her hungers, her rewards. She knows Jeanie at midnight, Jeanie in the morning. But there's something else she wants to know.

This time my fantasy. She rolls Jeanie over.

Your ass is mine.

memory, need,

MEMORY

trying to remember the feel of her skin between warm sheets, body smooth, skin brown from sun. she is taller than me, stronger too. she tells me of herself, old hurts, stories of the refugee camp and journeys by sea, stories of old lovers. her body is solid, her legs hold me up, her hips thrusting.

I remember running my teeth along her thighs, the tremor of her body, the welcome of lips parted in wetness. I rub my cheeks against her mound, pressing her thighs wider with my shoulders. my hands hold her ass, fingers tracing, grasping. my tongue flecks tender flesh, outer lips, slowly circling inward. I tease her lightly with my breath. she moans and how she moans. my heart and clit are beating in tune and I want to feel her come, to bury myself in her cunt.

my tongue slips between her lips, tasting her, knowing her pleasure, building a rhythm in the wave of her hips, in the pull of her thighs. sucking out her lips, my hands squeeze and slowly release. I am drawing myself into her as she begs. stroking her centre, I slip my fingers into her as she comes, deeper with every thrust.

she rests.

and desire

I lie cradled on her belly, a smile and the taste of her on my lips. she lifts me, rubbing her thighs against me, sucking at my breasts, tongue darting with the edge of her teeth. her hands are everywhere. she has pushed me back onto the bed, thighs streaming with wetness. she kisses me, hungry, hungry, but pulls away as I respond. her hands stroke my body, fingers dancing fire. she slips lower, from breast to belly and there, she's between my legs, teasing me as I lift my hips to her. she takes them easily, strong as she is. I don't know what she does, but I'm crying, full of her, tongue, hands, fingers dancing. I come flinging myself into her and she takes me to her rest.

NEED

she is thirty years old. this I know. smile is kind, hesitant. and beautiful. I think she thinks I am odd, an angry youngster, raging against the world. I puzzle her as she puzzles me.

she towers over me. yet she is uncertain, not knowing where I am coming from. and I can only wonder about her. is she or isn't she? what are her needs, her desires? will she turn me away?

I dream about her, dreams of hot sex and crumpled sheets, my lips on her soft breasts, along her strong thighs. I want to hear her cry out, her fingers slipping along my back, her tongue in my mouth, in my ears. I want and the wanting is urgent, painful.

her skin is brown, golden, for we are people of rice, fisherfolk and farmers, her arms strong, shoulders broad. I long to stroke the length of her back, to sink into her breasts, to fill my mouth with her nipples and roll my tongue stroke by stroke. I want to move against her, heart bursting, back arched, to see her eyes widen in surprise, pulled beyond, to this magical beginning, to feel her move, beyond herself, to feel her in me, in this wetness of salted honey, body loose, skin smooth, before everything I knew.

DESIRE

I want to nibble on your ears fuck you like you've never been fucked before suck your toes spread your thighs I want to make you come woman wild shouting begging for more I want to tongue your nipples trill on your clit rub the juices on my lips and kiss you in that wetness I want to fuck you woman like you've never been fucked before I want to rub up against you on the dance floor unzip your pants slip my hand inside in front of everyone I want them to know who you're going to fuck tonight I want to rip off your shirt rake my fingers down your back bite your thighs I want to kiss you long and hard my hand in your pussy fingers stroking your wetness I want to sit on your face and feel my juices over your nose mouth cheeks chin I want to cry out as your fingers fill me your mouth devouring I want to come knees weak hips wild laughter soft in darkness I want to hold you woman hold you and moan your name in my coming.

The

X stares at the row of titles: "Pussy Delight," "Best Erotica Of." What does it matter? What good will it do? Their relationship is over, dead and dry, dust in the proverbial wind. But she picks a book and frowns. What kind of book is this – "quixotic"? She thinks of windmills and doomed chivalry. Great, X sighs, the story of my life. Puts twenty bucks down and buys it anyway.

That night, in the bedroom, X pulls out the book as Y, yawning, settles in.

X reaches over. "I'll read to you."

And so X begins.

♀

Kathy Sato waits, rigid, in her father's truck, her black hair pulled back, silken strands carefully hidden by the baseball cap that squats on her head. She glances at the rearview mirror, checking, checking, and pops another stick of gum in her mouth. *Lower the voice*, she tells herself, *but spit it out before you say anything.* She worries about the truck, dented and scratched, if it is too big, or too hick, or too something. Kathy frets. Another glance in the mirror and she can see how young she is, and wonders if you can tell, if the eyes really are the windows of the soul. *But maybe*, she thinks, *maybe I can pass, they can't tell us apart*, and she tugs the cap on tighter. She can feel the roll of twenties in her jeans pocket, the bulk of her

Reader

oversized jacket, the binding around her breasts pinching. Her slender fingers grip the steering wheel as she peers across the street to the women working the corner. Jimmy Croydon had gone to the girls on this street, the braggart, and Kathy had done her research, read every trashy drugstore novel. She'd even stolen a copy of *Tropic of Cancer* by that Miller guy. Now or never, she thinks, biting her lip. She has never been out this late in this part of town. And the women in their tight clothes and short skirts – what if they see through her disguise, laugh at her, or follow her home. She can see her father's face, the slow shake of his head as he sighs. *But it's got to work*, Kathy whispers. *It's the only way I'll know.*

Kathy spits out her gum, takes a deep breath. Now or never. She puts the truck in gear and pulls out, down the drive.

♀

Christ, not another damned coming of age story and where is the sex anyway? X sighs. I need something more than this baby-dyke-bounces-through-the-boudoir tripe. But at least there is some character development between the bump and grind. As if an orgasm can change your life! How can we live up too all this hoopla? It's all romantic: sex and death and transcendental fucking. Waves and petals and all so repetitive. Maybe they'll be swallowed up by an earth shattering vaginal metaphor. It's all a diversion anyway, to keep us from thinking about environmental disasters and corporate scandals and the fascism of the New World Order, which is actually –

Y shifts, chiding, Leave the analysis at the door. Pleasure first. We can deal with the world later.

♀

The woman's name is Amber and although everything has gone as planned, Kathy's heart is racing, her palms stick to the steering wheel. Amber has given her a single glance and asked, "What'll it be?" just like in all the movies Kathy has seen. But she doesn't look sad–eyed or beaten, and Kathy shakes herself, all those clichés and expectations. Amber has slipped in beside her and off they go. Kathy, her voice pitched low, has asked her name. Her eyes had flickered as she said, "Amber. Now what'll it be?"

Kathy looks at Amber's smile, no meanness there. She turns onto a side street, to the park, beneath the quietness of trees, floating leaves. *Young*, she can see in Amber's eyes, but no suspicions. Kathy takes out her roll of twenties and hands them to Amber. "Th–there's a hundred there. In twenties. I . . . I hope that's enough."

Amber tucks her smile away, all business now. *This kid really wants it bad*, she thinks as she rolls the bills in her hand, not even counting, places them in her pocket, *It'll be quick.* She leans forward, and Kathy can see her skin glowing, as if her body were straining against her clothes, her breasts, tight against the thin fabric, or is it only her imagination, Kathy is not sure. Amber's hand goes out. To her surprise, Kathy catches it.

Kathy says, "I . . . I just want to touch." As Amber sits back, Kathy stammers, "I mean, if that's okay."

Amber smiles, tries to tuck it away. "Okay."

"Is, is there anywhere, I can't . . . I mean . . . not to touch. I mean . . . I want to kiss you . . . there." And Kathy glances down, her cheeks burning, and for a moment she hovers on the brink. *No, no, whatever you do, don't cry.*

Amber's voice brings her back. "That's okay." Her fingers lift

Kathy's chin and she is startled by her brown eyes, the dart of fear and desperation. Amber can see the wavering decision in her eyes, so clear, and softens. Kathy winces, but her trembling hands are reaching, holding Amber's breasts, encircling, enticing her nipples through the cloth, feeling the fullness of her grasp, her greedy hunger. Timidly, Kathy pulls up Amber's blouse, watches as she unhooks the bra, guides Kathy's mouth to this engulfing warmth. Kathy is kissing her, and kissing her, her mouth full of nipple, scent of soap and skin cream, and it feels so good, so good, tries to linger, can't, rushes head on. She takes, not so cautious now, reckless, her hands, as she wants, her body pressed against Amber, her mouth hungry kisses, taste of skin and she can smell her, rubs her nose in the scent. She tastes, mouth swallowing nipple popping out sucking tongue and Kathy can feel it, a burn between her legs slick and she wants to taste her there but not yet, her mouth tongue pressing against her, reckless now, bump and push and pull, her head brushing the roof of the truck as her cap falls off and hair spills across shoulders, once carefully hidden, a moment's shock as she realizes the ruse is over, and throws herself back. *Oh god sweet Jesus.* A wave of self-hatred so deep it drowns her *fuck you idiot* as she tries to catch the cap push back her hair, too late scuttling away from her *sorry I'm sorry* her tears as Amber stares and stares. Kathy's words choke back the sobs inside her *dyke loser queer* stabs them to feel the pain better than the humiliation, this woman staring at her. Couldn't even pay her enough, no, not for a perv like her.

Amber's hand reaches out, strokes back the long black hair to the face hidden below. "Sweetheart," she murmurs, "it's okay." She is young, she must be young, this charade, such open tears. She holds her as the buried face slowly rises.

"You think I'm a freak, don't you?"

Amber sighs. "No."

Kathy bites her lip. "I'm not . . . I'm not a guy." She holds her breath, waiting for the bolt to fall.

Amber bursts out laughing, in spite of herself. "No kidding!"

After a glance at Kathy, she's subdued. "It's okay. Come on, let's get some coffee."

♀

Oh, no! Not a hooker with a heart of gold!
  Shhh.
  But —
  Shhh. Just read.

♀

At Tim Hortons, in front of a French cruller, Kathy tells Amber about the truck, her father, the lie of staying over at her cousin's for the weekend. She tells of the years of crushes, a kiss in fifth grade from Laura Buterson, staring down Miss Hilton's cleavage in English 11. She tells her of the days of mowing lawns, clipping hedges, the afternoons of babysitting and errands for the twenties in Amber's pocket, the rolled coins and pop bottles. She tells her of her fumbled dreams, the furtive burn inside her.

At the end of it, Amber taps her fingers. "Well, I can't say I know very much about all this. If you want to know the truth I don't go that way. But I can point you in the right direction. A friend of mine has a house in the east end. She's what you'd call a kindred spirit. I'll take you there."

"Thank you," Kathy mumbles, and she bows her head, willing the tears not to come. Amber's hand is on hers, a simple warmth of touch, and she gazes into Amber's face. In the light of Tim Hortons Kathy can see she looks older than under the street lights. She can hear the snicker of the men in the corner at Amber's short skirt and high heels, but they can't see her eyes. "Thank you," Kathy says clearly, her voice ringing through the smoke and stale coffee, "thank you," grasping Amber's hand.

"Hey, been there. Or somewhere like that. I think we all have."

♀

The old Victorian sits at the end of Winchester street. Its spires are modest, the gables, hushed, and ivy creeps up the fading red brick. A sprawling oak tree shades the front, and the yard slopes to the river. The driveway is long, the house set back in the lot. Kathy parks the truck in the drive. Her hands clutch the steering wheel. Amber smiles and nods towards the entrance.

Amber knocks and the heavy oak door opens to a small light-haired woman, dressed formally in a gentleman's suit and tie. Kathy is surprised, but only twists her cap in her hands. Amber asks for "Ruby," and they are sent into the waiting room, full of stuffed leather chairs and dark polished wood. A typewriter sits on a desk in the corner and bookshelves line the walls. Kathy stares. A mirror glances back at her, reflecting herself, the room, the doorway. An orchid blooms on the table, luminous against the mahogany, and calla lilies glow on the mantle.

"Ruby!" Amber dashes up to the woman in the doorway. Kathy glances away as Amber nods towards her, feels the eyes of Ruby sweep over her. As they whisper, Kathy gazes at Ruby in the mirror. The only word Kathy can find for her is handsome, handsome in her black slacks and low-cut vest. Her hair is long and black, her lips painted red, her skin, a tawny glow. Kathy shivers and her knees feel weak. Amber's laughter is soft as Kathy turns to face them, sees Amber pass half of the roll of twenties to the woman with the painted lips. Amber winks a catch–you–later smile and she is out the door.

Kathy shifts as Ruby approaches, tries not to stare at the swell of breasts, for it's not a vest after all, but a black lacy bodice. Ruby takes in her glance and laughs at Kathy's flushing cheeks, smiles. "Welcome. We are a clubhouse, a special kind of clubhouse. My name is Ruby." She takes her hand.

"I'm Kathy."

"Let's take off that jacket and get you into a hot bath before we get started."

"G–get started?"

Ruby smiles and with a gesture, a woman appears. "Jules will show you the way."

♀

Kathy is shown into the Red Room, and she stumbles by the door. Inside, there is a four–poster bed draped in scarlet velvet. Jules brushes past her, places a small tin tub in the centre of the room, and stokes the flames in the fireplace as the damp wood crackles and spits. Kathy looks out the window, sees Amber walking down the drive. *What will happen now?* she wonders. *What is happening now?*

"J–Jules?"

"Yes?" Jules turns, pushing back blonde strands from her eyes. "Oh, let me get that off," and pulls the bulky jacket from Kathy's shoulders.

"What's happening. I mean, what are you doing?"

Jules rolls her eyes. "Giving you a bath." Kathy stares at the flat shallow tub that barely reaches her knees. "You'll see what I mean. Now come on, off with that."

Kathy crosses her arms, but a dark flush gives her away. "I can bathe myself. I'm not a child."

"You heard what Ruby said. I'm giving you a bath. She's very particular about these kinds of things. No, don't touch." Jules smacks away Kathy's hands as they begin unbuckling her belt. "I do this. Think of it as my job."

With a tug the belt snakes out of its loops, buttons slip from their holes, but Kathy remembers the pinch around her chest and blushes. Jules smiles as she pulls the shirt away, frowns at the make–shift binding. She gently unfurls Kathy's body from the rough cloth. Jules is silent as she works, pulls down jeans, panties, and guides Kathy to the tub. A knock on the door, and it opens to a woman carrying a jug of steaming water, and then another. Jules works silently, as she pours the water on a cloth, gently rubs Kathy's feet in the tub, working upwards, caressing, especially tender along her breasts, the lines where the cloth pressed into her flesh, working, kneading, stroking, splashing with the steaming water, bottom to top. *What does it mean when a woman bathes you?* Kathy, breathing deeply, her body tense, but still she has to stand, her arms, the slightest tremor, as she wants to grasp, to hold. God, she feels herself wet under this woman's hands. *Please please don't let her know.* Another knock, as a woman brings a bar of soap, with fresh towels and a handful of scented candles. Jules, working with the soap now, a stronger massage, her fingers digging into muscle up the calves, between the thighs, finger sudsy, foamy, sticky as she strokes a teasing lather and Kathy, the sharp intake of her breath, as she's swirling deeper, a rasping moan, as she's rubbing her, not enough, not enough, but slick as she moves behind, her hands on ass, Kathy's blush *is it shame or desire* the sudden *oh my god* as a finger slips inside, the other orifice, no, never thought she would be there, but pops out so soon, too soon, hands on belly up to breasts slippery, but no she doesn't tweak the nipples up to the neck and gently as she covers the face.

Shock of water against her body as she shudders, the towel wiping the eyes. Kathy opens them and Jules is gone.

♀

A knock on the door and Kathy sits up on the velvet bed. Naked, she is self-conscious, the jeans and jacket taken away long before. Ruby stands by the door, holding out a silk robe. Kathy crosses her legs, she's still wet from Jules and thinks Ruby knows this. But Ruby only says, "Come," and Kathy obeys her.

In her silk robe Kathy can feel the air roaming around her thighs, floating, going down the stairs, the robe slipping open, just a glance, and the women, so many women, below her looking up, between her legs. Kathy burns, her nipples hardening, and they can see this too, the silk falls against her body, caresses with each step. So many women, different races and sizes, so many, as they make their way across the room, but Kathy can feel their hands in the crush of bodies, a stroke across a breast, a pinch of the nipple.

Different smells, and her head is spinning, but there, a hand between her thighs, caressing through the silk. Ruby pulls her through, murmuring into her ear. But is it her hands? Too late, and Kathy steps into the mirror room and stands gazing into herself.

In the mirror room there are sixteen mirrors, all focused on the central dais. There is one light that falls, illuminating only this platform. The mirrors feed on this light, reflecting themselves, reflecting.

Kathy's knees are weak. She wants, and the wanting burns, touched by so many hands, she craves release, but how, she does not quite know how. Ruby takes her to the dais. Ruby knows how. Ruby will show her. The silken robe has fallen and Ruby is kissing her slowly. Kathy has tried to press up against her, but Ruby has pushed her back. *Let go*, Ruby whispers, *let go* and kisses her deep. Kathy is melting almost to tears, Ruby's hands, fingers, Kathy can feel them all over, and closes her eyes. Her mouth on her breasts, as Kathy arches her back, nails along her belly and toes, tongue between her toes. Kathy's mind blinks, a sudden confusion, as *how could? how could?* flashes through her mind. Her eyes open and she sees Ruby standing back, watching her pleasure and these women, *five women*, suckling at Kathy's breasts, fingers, toes. Her senses slice open, the murmur of voices in the dark *I'm being watched* as she stares at Ruby, *all the women in the hallway. Oh god!* she cries out.

Ruby waves and the five women drop back. Kathy, without the mouths, fingers, caresses, falls, her cunt throbbing. She clutches her legs together and rocks. She stares in tears at Ruby, handsome Ruby. Ruby does not smile. She sits down on the dais and whispers into her ear.

"Kathy, do you know what you want? Will I show you?" Kathy's tears swell in her throat, she cannot say, does not know the words. She is new, too new to this, the hum of sensations in her blood. She wants to say *touch me*, to whisper *fuck me*, but fear darts along her spine, catches in her lungs. Ruby pulls Jules to the dais, places her alongside Kathy. With one strong move, Ruby tears Jules' bodice, right down the middle, leaving her exposed. "Ah," Ruby murmurs, "you're wet already." Ruby spreads Jules' legs wide, sees her shiver, her hands gripping for whatever she can. She smells her wetness, lingers over the tangled patch of hair. She doesn't see the tears in Jules' eyes, nor the whispered thanks she imparts to Kathy, but she does see the twitches as Ruby blows softly, softly over Jules's swollen clit, her hips raised so very eagerly to meet that skillful, teasing tongue. And when Ruby dives, Jules is begging her, Jules, who has never raised her voice, screams she's being banged to kingdom come.

Kathy sits watching, so wet, squirming in her wetness, she's never been this wet before. She is dying to touch herself, but knows Ruby's punishment would be too terrible. She wants so badly her breasts ache, her cunt is curling up inside her. She sees Jules' pleasure, knows this is something she must learn, chafes at the closeness of it. She sees Jules come, and come, and come, the glistening wetness on Ruby's lips, tongue, rolling down her chin, she wants to open herself to Ruby, to swallow her, and waits, knowing she'll be the one.

♀

There's a buzz in the dining hall. The women know something's up. Jules steeps in the glow of her after-fuck. She lies on the table and women stroke her, some nibble on her clit, suck at her breasts, and she comes weakly, drunk on the taste of her pleasure. She's the first fuck of the evening, open to everyone.

At the second table, Kathy sits with Ruby. Kathy stares at Jules, legs spread, an open meal. "I'm surprised she's able to move," Kathy murmurs.

"Tomorrow she won't be able to," Ruby replies. "She could teach you a lot."

"How, how could you do that? Give her to all those women? It's you she wants, you can tell . . ." Kathy falters, ". . . by the look in her eyes."

"There are rules here, just like any other house. You've got to work your way up. It's not just about buying your way in."

"What about me? Did I buy my way in?"

Ruby frowns. "I'm a teacher." She stares at the table full of rice, roasted chicken, salad, the plates of vegetables, the wine. "Sex is like food. Sex nourishes, keeps you strong, feeds the soul." She takes a cob of corn, slathers the pebbled surface with glistening butter. "And we all have an appetite." Ruby walks over to Jules, who's being eaten out by a red-haired woman. A firm tap and the woman steps away.

Jules, on the brink, takes time coming down.

Ruby leads Jules to the table, sits her between Kathy and herself. The bodice is open and Kathy can only stare. She has never been so close to a woman, this aroused, this open. Ruby begins caressing Jules' pubic hair and Kathy can smell her, longs to taste. "Have you ever made love to a woman?" Ruby asks.

"No."

"Well, that was your first lesson. Going down, cunnilingus. The next lesson will be penetration. Fingers, dildos, anything will do, as long as you know her limitations, that it's safe, and you have enough lubrication. Safety is an issue. You've got to have trust." Jules' legs part and Ruby's caressing circle goes deeper. Ruby whispers, "Can she eat you?"

Jules offers a soft moaning yes.

Ruby looks at Kathy, but Kathy is disbelieving. She sees Ruby's fingers part those lips, the pink wetness of kisses and she wants to but holds herself back. Ruby's fingers come away, a deep groan from Jules as she tries to lift her hips, to catch those fingers, Ruby's sticky fingers. "You want to fuck her, taste her," Ruby whispers to Kathy. "Smell her. Feast your eyes. You never have, have you? Look at what those lips are saying."

Kathy is drawn down to the honey. She cannot wait, tells herself of Jules' need, but feels her own raging hungers, flicks the tip of her tongue against Jules' luscious slit, thinks of succulents, the tangy burst of pulp and sweet juices in her mouth. Kathy stares, thinks *she's so wet* as Jules bucks against her, demanding more, more from those dawdling lips, her cries sharper as Kathy takes the plunge and sucks and licks and nibbles. Kathy feels a stabbing bolt of joy run through her as she rolls those soft warm musky lips, sucks the budding clit, loses herself in a rhythm of tongue over clit, her hands gripping Jules' ass, holding her cunt up, swallowing her, tongue inside that wetness slurping juices licketysplit, those hips bucking against her, crying *please please pleasepleaseplease* on the brink she can feel it, wants to feel Jules come in her face, thighs gripping her, she's earned it – but Ruby pulls her away, cunt juice running down her chin, Jules' cry of pain as cool air rushes in absence, Ruby pulling Jules' legs wider, cunt open, the corn sliding into her, creamy butter wetness, Jules' scream higher into *yesyesfuckmechristfuckmore* as the corn cob plunges deep in out cunt squeezing it to cream corn pussy juice Ruby pumping it riding hips *fuck fuck* screaming until Jules comes, crying, sobbing spasms making her legs a puddle. Ruby holds her, gently slipping the corn cob out of her cunt lips, so spent she's asleep in Ruby's arms. Ruby eating the corn on the cob, rolling the kernels on her tongue, popping them as she swallows.

♀

Kathy sits at the table. The taste of Jules is still on her lips and a dull ache gnaws at her. It has slipped from the surface of her cunt, burning through her vaginal walls, burrowing deep like some coiled searing beast. No one has touched her there, gone inside, and she craves it, her need ripples through her body. Her nipples, pert, are insistent and the very air makes her twitch. She could throw herself to any stranger in this hall, yet knows no woman would take her. Ruby must take her. Ruby must mark her pussy, hear her screams, must make her beg. Kathy tries to quiet her mind, to push away the fantasies, the torments from her body. She waits. When Ruby bends over Jules, Kathy can see the round firm ass, the silkiness tightening between her legs, the shape of Ruby's cunt lips. She has waited so long, through girlfriends who would turn away, the whispered jeers of schoolmates. Too long, she has waited too long.

Kathy slips out of the dining room. She wants a quiet room to touch herself, to release this keening lust that's eating her alive. Even the act of walking torments her, the slightest rub of those swollen lips, the robe caressing her breasts like a hand. Kathy knows the wetness has dripped down her thighs, craves to touch the women in the hall. She opens curtain after curtain in a corridor without locks. Behind the velvet plush, a woman, spread open, pussy glistening, a multitude of hands, tongues, mouths stroking, sucking, drinking her to pleasure. In another, two entwined. A woman on her back, moaning with every thrust as she is ridden, a leather strap pulled across the hips of the other, legs draped over shoulders. Curtain after curtain, Kathy can hear the ecstasy, smell the pungent flow of cunt juice. Tears roll down her cheeks, until she stumbles across a door. And opens into a dark cavernous room.

Kathy has a moment's vertigo, as she thinks *mirror room*, but there are no mirrors here. Her attention is caught by a scene in the centre of the room, a woman bound in a leather sling, legs spread open. She is on the verge, begging, begging as three fingers slowly enter and retreat, a mocking indolent fuck that stops, starts, stops, the woman, straining, her vaginal muscles contracting, but no, her partner's fingers pop out. The woman tries to make herself come, the press and release of thighs, of lips, so desperately. *Please please make me, make me come, please fuck.* But her partner takes another woman, spreads her open in front of her, and begins the dance of tongue and clit. The bound woman watches, her hips thrusting from the sling, but she slips back, always slips back, she cannot touch herself, fingers too far, the leather too strong. She watches as the other woman is fucked spread open, watches as they twist, as the other is pumped from the front, fist hammering in out in, an *oh oh oh* thrust as if from that convulsing cunt, now a fuck from behind, as she watches, desire sinking into her blood, into her bones. She stares, mouth open as the other woman comes, screaming, she can see the spasms, smells the cunt cream, maybe even tastes the spray of juices. Her partner stands as the women crowd the door. Her arm is dripping with wet. A chaste kiss for the bound woman, only one, and she drapes a kerchief over the tortured pussy. She exits, leaving her high and dry.

The bound woman sobs. She presses her pussy muscles, clutches at nothing. She closes her eyes.

Kathy walks into the pool of light. She stares at this woman. She slips the kerchief off her sex, clit still inflamed. She wants to suck this woman, feels Jules on her tongue. *What is happening to me?*

The woman's eyes flutter open.

"Water."

Kathy finds the water bottle by the bed in the corner. She places the bottle to the woman's mouth, holds it as she gulps in small mouthfuls. Carefully Kathy unties the bonds to the sling. The woman's legs ease down, shaking. Kathy takes her to the low bed, watches her sink into the sheets. Tenderly Kathy pushes back the sweat-soaked hair.

The woman smiles. "Thank you." She drinks. The bottle shakes in her hand. "My name is . . . Sabina."

"Kathy."

Kathy flushes in confusion. She wants pussy, does not want to ask, knows the woman's exhaustion, and feels the urge to fuck her. "How long have you been in that strap thing?"

"Two days," Sabina says bitterly, "two days of fucking and never letting me come. God, I'm sore." She opens her legs to delicate curls and folds and Kathy feels her own cunt jump.

"Two days! Do you want anything to eat . . . we could go to the dining –"

"I've been fucked by carrots and cucumbers. I've eaten mangoes shoved in pussies, cunt-dipped bananas, slurping cream off tits. And everything on that rack over there," she nods towards the corner, lies back on crisp linen sheets, "I've been fucked inside and out." She tries to sit up, fails. Blushing, she asks, "Could you . . . could you pull it out of me?"

"Sorry?"

Sabina rolls over and Kathy can see her round cream cheeks, her puckered asshole. And out of the hole a string dangles, a loop at the end. "They're anal beads. Could you pull them? I can't seem to reach."

Kathy reaches for the loop and peers closely. She gives them a soft tug and Sabina jerks, ass high in the air, not so eager to let them go. Slowly, slowly Kathy pulls the metal balls out, six balls on the string. As they plop out, they each give a metal *dong* and Kathy can see Sabina's ass contract, as if to suck the shiny sphere back in, the sense of loss each ball engenders, the asshole pushing open and close, wave after wave, as each *dong dong dong* spills out of her. The anal beads out, Sabina sighs. Kathy can see the viscous juice seep from Sabina's pussy. *Will she let me fuck her now?*

Sabina turns. "Thank you for taking me out. Did you see me? Did you see me all laid out like that?"

"Yes."

"Would you have fucked me? You wouldn't have left me dangling."

Kathy stares at the open pussy, her mouth drawn magnetically. "No, I mean, yes, you're so beautiful, all those little curls. . . ."

Sabina closes her legs. "Will . . . will you fuck me? Fuck me to the finish?"

Kathy smiles and kisses her, smells the damp sweat and feels the wetness as she presses her thigh against Sabina's mound. Sabina falls back, open. Joy flutters in Kathy's chest, every cell in her body electric. Kathy kisses and kisses, bites and kisses, twirling Sabina's nipple in her mouth, flicking tongue, even as her fingers find Sabina's sore and tender lips, parts them, as Kathy slips down, thinks honeycombs and nectar, feels the jerk of Sabina's body as she sucks the engorged clit, Sabina's cries, her fingers in Kathy's hair as she licks and suckles, nibbles and rubs, *two days of this*, feeling the build in hips, as her tongue races, riding the wave of contractions, her face awash in cunt cum, lapping, her face mashed inside, Kathy swallowing Sabina's cunt or Sabina engulfing her, she rides, Sabina's hands smacking the bed as she comes, Kathy's chin grazing the tangled mound *fuck fuck fuck* her orgasm fading, Sabina's thighs slapping Kathy's head as she licks the traces of pleasure, Kathy does not let her go, her tongue rooting deep into those folds, this banquet of pussy gluttonous ravenous Sabina's *please please please* going deeper thinks of Ruby's red tongue wants to fuck her till she begs Sabina's scream fuck as she comes again, tears and cunt juice racking sob of Sabina's *yes yes yes* sheets sticky grabbed into Sabina's fists as she arches and falls Kathy rides her until she is finished cannot bear even the breath of air above those pussy lips Kathy gasping lying beside her *god I've fucked her* and tenderly tenderly sweeps back her hair.

Kathy lies back, licks her lips, cannot get enough of this. The sheets cool against her flaming skin, she thinks *second wind* as she gulps the air and feels a breeze stroking her own swollen need. She sits up on her elbows, wants to place Sabina's hand between her legs, a thrill of delight, of anticipation, a childish squeal of *my turn my turn* ready to spill out of her. But Sabina turns, eyes lowered, asks. "Could you fuck me again?"

Two days, fucked for two days, rings through Kathy's mind, she can see Sabina's pussy hanging, this loveliness, so ripe and ready, a furrow ringed with sodden curls. Kathy's cunt just clenches, cannot release. Kathy sighs and Sabina smiles knowingly, and gestures to the rack by the wall. Kathy wheels the rack around, as part of her wails *my turn my turn!* pulls off the concealing sheet to reveal the harness and straps, the multicoloured dildos, the strange devices of plastic and rubber, the bowls of thick clear liquid, metals clips linked by tiny gossamer chain.

Sabina blushes, "Fingers first." Kathy is at a loss, she's never done this, what is Sabina asking for? She thinks of Ruby and the corn on the cob and traces the outline of Sabina's vaginal lips, the little button clitoris that protrudes from Sabina's dampened bush. She remembers the bath tub and Jules' circular caress, beginning there, brushing the triangle patch, rubbing deeper and deeper. Sabina rolls her hips. Kathy is getting the hang of it.

Kathy, ever the student, wants to see, hear, taste. She sinks to the foot of the bed, between Sabina's legs, sees, as she strokes that little button, how Sabina's limbs flail, hands grasping, legs bucking, as if for some hold, some purchase. Kathy's finger dips in, plays with the wetness, the sound of her finger sticky–stick like the plip–plop of rain. Kathy can see the sex flush between Sabina's legs, the clit rising as she teases it out, the pinkness of Sabina's hole. Her finger swims in, so warm, so moist, so close, the vaginal walls so strong that she slides two fingers, Sabina's cunt, all muscle as she tries to hold her, Kathy's twirling swirling fingers pulling in out fast slow, Sabina's hips trying to catch her, Sabina's voice rising, Kathy is mesmerized, sinks her fingers, three now, thinks of the corn, of the butter. She pulls out completely and Sabina whimpers, clutches her hands over the emptiness.

Please.

Kathy scoops a handful of lube from the bowl, slips her finger inside, first one, then two, then three, filling Sabina, churning the wetness, bubbly frothy cunt cum spilling over lips, down sliding into crack hole, sheet staining puddle. She slips her fourth finger in, feels Sabina's cunt close around her knuckles, strokes thumb over the rosy bud, waves her hand inside. In. Out. In. Kathy slips her fingers out to below the knuckles, tucks in her thumb, pushes gently, sees her hand disappear into Sabina, the whole pumping fuck of her hand, Sabina's moan so deep, as if it's dragged out of her womb as she comes, her whole body twisting, racking, Kathy's hand, feeling wave after wave of contractions, she cannot pull out but pumps deeper her mouth descending on that stubborn pulsing clit as she flips her over the edge, Sabina sobbing, her body falling to the bed, gasping, in a torpid haze.

Kathy waits, her hand locked in Sabina's pussy. She feels Sabina's descent, her flush into languor. With her other hand she cups the lubricant, pours into her lips and inch by inch, slips herself free. Sabina's eyes open and Kathy stares. Sabina's eyes are the deepest green and Kathy cannot read them, they are so cloudy, so heavy. As if in reply Sabina takes Kathy's hand, dips fingers into the thick liquid of the bowl, and guides them to her tiny puckered asshole, rosy red and waiting. *Fuck me until I'm full of you.* Kathy slowly, cautiously presses her finger in out of her, feels a tightness different from her sticky cunthole. She feels Sabina moving against her and swirls her finger inside. Sabina's asshole sucks her in, but Kathy resists the pull. Sabina's mouth opens with every touch, Kathy's finger forcing out a gasp, a moan, a ragged keening *fuck*. Kathy works this bottom, learning to plunge and tease, pulling out completely just to hear Sabina plead. Kathy opens Sabina's ass crack, examines the precious hole, now creamy with lube. She wants to kiss it but doesn't know if she should. Her tongue darts out. Sabina gasps and that's all Kathy needs to know. She traces the ridge with her tongue slip–sliding deeper, spreading the cheeks wide for her hunger, hands full of ass, rimming the edge, ramming her tongue, her tongue fucking her asshole, Kathy's teeth marks on Sabina's cheeks. She falls on Sabina, her hips slamming into her ass, she wants to fuck her like a woman, to fill every crevice of her and leave her mark. Kathy stands, the ache in her own cunt goading her on, pulls Sabina up on her knees. She stares at the rack, the Y chain of three tiny pinchers, and takes them in her hand. Roughly she pulls apart Sabina's legs, grabs her breasts from behind, her fingers working her tips into a frenzy, Sabina's head rocking back and swiftly Kathy clamps those twisting pinchers onto those red puffed nipples, Sabina's scream as she falls forward onto hands and knees, but Kathy's faster, her fingers diving into her cunt from behind as Sabina bends, so open, so exposed, leans forward, driving deep as Sabina tries to twist away, but no, pussy lips pummeled, a yank of the chain as Sabina snaps up on her knees, the loss of Kathy's fingers pull away, as Kathy reaches around, snaps that third tiny clip to Sabina's sore swollen clit, Sabina's howl of fury now as Kathy tugs, tears running as Kathy takes from the rack two dildos and shoves one into Sabina's asshole, another into her cunt. She pumps two different rhythms and her teeth yank at the chain. A slip of the dildo and she grips harder, she feels it buzzing in her hand and Sabina thrusts wildly, madly. She stares at the instrument and twists the handle, the vibration shooting stronger up through her arm. Sabina's legs are flailing and she is begging, pleading. Kathy pulls out the vibrating toy, presses it against clit and Sabina jumps, sobbing. Kathy pulls out the dildos, sees Sabina writhing on the cunt–smeared bed, so open. She takes a harness from the rack, adjusts it to her hips, slips a dildo in the ring, a thick dick with a vibrating clit tickler, solid against her pelvis, and a butt plug from the shelf. But before she can even turn, Sabina is there, *sucking the dildo in her harness!* Kathy stands in shock. She can see Sabina's tongue slick along the silicone, teasing and licking, but gasps as *Sabina takes it into her mouth.* Kathy shivers, her legs almost buckle. *So this it what it's like to be blown.* She doesn't understand the rush she feels as she pushes Sabina down, the need to fuck her, to fill her, no preliminaries, thighs apart and she dives. The buzzer is on full blast, she can feel the vibration but it's in the wrong spot for her. Sabina cries, feels as though she's splitting open, her skin on fire, her womb is burning, she feels the earth turning as Kathy takes her from the front, the *oh oh oh* of cries as Kathy opens up her ass, shoves the ass dick inside. Sabina feels, Sabina feels, the animal rutting of Kathy's passion *fuck me fuck me* as she comes, the stinging *buzzbuzz* as the dick does not let her go, Kathy still thrusting Sabina's tears and wetness the final cunt stabs ripples of pain laced with pleasure she comes and body falls into a blessed blissed–out sleep.

Kathy pulls out of her, turns off the buzzer, steps out of the harness. She stares at Sabina, slumps to the floor. She hears, does not see Ruby, who begins a slow clap, as the audience joins in. The house lights come up and it is the mirror room behind the curtains, the platform, the dais. And the women. The whistles and cheers. Ruby comes forward but she's too late. Kathy has fainted.

♀

When Kathy wakes she is in the Red Room, in a long narrow bathtub, floating in sudsy, soapy water. She remembers this room, Jules in the dining hall, Sabina spread on the low platform bed, and thanks heaven she's had the presence of mind to pass out. She closes her eyes, feels the lapping water like a caress, silky smooth, like a finger teasing her cunt lips – and bolts, turns to see Ruby in the bath behind her, arms slinking around. Kathy rises, unsteadily. Ruby gazes at her, smiles at the pussy hair ringed with bubbles. She pulls the plug, takes the shower head in hand. "Rinse?"

Kathy looks around, no clothes, no towels – the keys to her truck in the pocket of her jeans. She sees the champagne bottle nestled in ice beside the bathtub – a victory celebration? But not for her. She takes Ruby's hand, a truce, and Ruby pulls her down. As Ruby passes the shower head over her, splashes off the suds, she asks, "Have you ever seen yourself?"

Kathy does not trust her voice, turns her face away.

"Your pussy." Ruby notes the blush and smiles. "I'll teach you." At the end of the rinse Ruby calls for a mirror and Jules, smiling, comes forward, a large oval mirror in hand.

"Sit with us," Ruby commands, "in the front." Jules slips into the tub, mirror in hand, and Kathy sees herself, with Ruby behind her. "Lean back," Ruby whispers, as she drapes Kathy's legs over each side of the tub. Kathy stares at herself, so exposed, sees Ruby's fingers trace her lips, sees Jules smiling at the sight of her. Ruby begins rubbing the mound of hair. "Mons veneris." Kathy's dark hairs glisten, so newly wet. Ruby's fingers sink down, along the sides of lips as she glides "Labia majora," and Kathy cannot help it, the slickness as Ruby strokes, opening "Labia minora," so pink she wants a mouth there to sip the dewy sweetness as her hips to rock forward for more. Kathy stares at those fingers, unfurling those petals. A bite at her ear as Ruby warns, "Pay attention, there'll be test for this – vagina." And in – her finger, a whelp from Kathy, bucking forward as she feels Ruby slipping in and out, the viscous liquid sticking, she sees herself coming, Jules' smile as she licks her lips, but Ruby pulls up, away, fingers covered in pussy juice. Kathy is helpless, all revealed, she can't think beyond her cunt. A sharp slap between Kathy's legs as admonishment makes her wetter still. "Clitoris," Ruby draws out the sibilance, and tips of her fingers swirl around the hood, but always Ruby pulls away, splashing the shower head across breasts, thighs.

Kathy moans.

Ruby smiles, pinches Kathy's clit, smiles as Kathy twitches.

"Good. Good." Ruby places her hands between Kathy's legs. "Do you know what this is? My snatch. My pussy. I'll fuck you, Kathy. You're mine, remember that. I'll open you so wide and I'll dive right in, burn every inch of you, every nook and every cranny. I'll fuck you hard and on my terms and everyone who comes afterwards will know you're mine." Ruby's hand rubbing, tugging the hairs of Kathy's pussy. "Do you want that, Kathy? Do you want me to fuck you?"

Kathy closes her eyes, she fights it, but she sinks deeper every time. "Yes. I want it. I want you to fuck me."

Ruby's hand reaches for the champagne bucket. As Kathy opens her eyes, she feels it, the shock of ice on her clitoris making her leap, another kind of burning, as Ruby holds her, slides the coldness along her lips, into her cunt, but she bucks and the cubes slip down the drain. Ruby parts her legs wider, turns the shower head on to stream, splashes it down between Kathy's legs, a soft caressing wash and Kathy, in confusion, does not know that Ruby can fuck her in this way, lies back, but feels the beading water thump thump thump her clit she cries *oh* but she wants to be fucked, fucked by Ruby, the water pushing her thump thump

thump to the brink but this time it's Ruby lifting her out of the tub, Kathy's cries of *pleasepleaseplease* a rising desperation as she tries to rub herself against Ruby's thigh, Ruby throwing her to the bed, holding her until her thrashing passes, exhausted into tears. Kathy, feeling the hollowness of her cunt, knows it rides her, curls into Ruby's arms and weeps. *Oh god please please.*

"Soon," Ruby promises, "soon."

♀

Kathy wakes, again in the Red Room. She is naked on the bed and Ruby lies, asleep, beside her. The bucket of ice and champagne are gone, the bathtub, moved to the corner. The mirror stands at the foot of the bed and there are no clothes for her, no robes. Kathy gazes at Ruby, asleep. She stares at the rise of breasts, traces the bump of nipples, cups them in her hands. Ruby stirs. Kathy wants to fuck her in her dreams, make her wet as she sleeps. She strokes Ruby's thighs open, steals between her legs. She places her mouth to Ruby's mound and kisses, floats, kisses, floats up to breasts, hovers as her face rubs her soft giving flesh, searching out the nipple bumps to suck through the fabric. Kathy stares, wants so fiercely to slip under the lace, caressing the crotch, to make out her clit, the curve of her lips, the dip as she sighs. Kathy wants her naked, feels the ache pulse in her cunt and begins tearing the fragile lace, patch by patch, lifts it away. She has never seen Ruby like this, chokes at the sight of her – the bushy hair between her legs, the solidness of breasts, so beautiful, so sublime. She nudges apart Ruby's legs, stares, smelling the heavy musk of her, tickling hairs as her tongue parts those lips, her clit standing, as she sucks it, sweet, like a persimmon or a pearl, she feels a hand in her hair, as Ruby sighs, lifting her, a chuckle, "I can't leave you alone for a minute, can I?"

"I . . . I just wanted. . . ."

"I know." Ruby presses closer. "I want to fuck you too." And Ruby kisses her, her hands in her hair, Kathy's long silken hair, and Ruby's mouth, feasting on her, tongue, over lips over tongue down to breasts, gobbling her nipples, as she pushes open those thighs, Ruby's hand gliding down, feeling the wetness of her, the hot sticky nectar calling, Ruby wants to crawl inside – but Kathy grabs her fingers, holds them. Ruby pulls away. "What is it, Kathy? Don't you want this?"

"I . . . I," Kathy stammers, "I'm a virgin. I mean, I . . . don't know what I mean."

Ruby smiles, thinks, despite the dildo and clamps, Kathy's still an apprentice, never been fucked. Well, penetrated, yes, and played with, but not truly and deeply fucked.

"Do you want to take it slow?"

"Yes. Please."

"What do you want?"

Kathy blushes, her cunt shivering as she hears this. "I . . . I want . . . maybe, on top and . . . you, I mean, the oral sex thing." The last words falling to a whisper.

"You want to sit on my face," Ruby smiles. "See, in the mirror."

Ruby lies down, sees Kathy, so skittish, as she tries to straddle. Ruby grips her hips, lowers her, sees the illusion of control fade from Kathy's eyes. Ruby watches Kathy as she catches herself in the mirror. A flick of Ruby's tongue, and the mirror's forgotten, a gasp and shiver, Kathy does not know how to hold this stance, but Ruby's hands are strong. Ruby inhales her, glides over clit, lips, skims the mound and teases. She eats Kathy, sucking cunt soft juicy slip slurp of pussy guzzling salt sweetness this drinking pleasure. Kathy, rocking, cannot hold herself anymore, hears a low whimper, hears herself, sobs as Ruby bites her thigh, wants to pull away but Ruby grips tightly, feels the struggle the sob beg of *please Ruby please*. Kathy feels a smile pressing into her cunt, a tongue fucking her, delving into folds of lips, sucking and spreading, her clit rising out of its hood, the sensations radiating from that centre Ruby's teeth tongue lips gnawing at the bud, eating her, licking back, Ruby biting into fruit, spurt of juices, rolling the hard seed on her tongue. Kathy looks down at her *Ruby Ruby Ruby* feels the first pull contraction *too much too fast* wants to hold it and closes her eyes. Ruby reaches up and tweaks her nipple, her hand around the rim of Kathy's sweet virgin ass as her finger pokes in the shock of it tilting cunt forward clit sliding into Ruby's mouth ferocious suck suck suck as Kathy screams pain and joy and clit on fire she comes, body racked, even Ruby cannot hold her. She tumbles to the bed but Ruby follows her, mouth still hungry, not yet sated, her tongue driving deeper, a long tongue kiss lapping and she pauses for breath, Kathy's pussy exposed below her, open thighs.

Kathy, beneath her, stares into heaven. They have fallen, tangled. Ruby's pussy is just above Kathy's face, the scent makes her head spin, her mouth water. Kathy stares at those closed labia, wants to taste the nectar that must be there, to open her cunt and gaze into her glistening. Kathy jumps, Ruby's tongue inside her *how can it get so deep?* She gazes at the pussy dangling above her and cannot wait, shoves her face into Ruby, tongue diving into cunthole, drinks the juice inside those lips, sucking, she feels Ruby's clitoris leap *oh god she wants it, wants me to fuck her* and feels a stinging slap between her legs as Ruby pulls away, off the bed, to the bureau by the window.

When Ruby turns back Kathy sees the pink flush on her cheeks and she knows something different is happening. Ruby is not smiling. The Y chain with the tiny clamps are in her hand. Kathy sees them, thinks of Sabina and squirms. Ruby grabs her ass cheeks, pulls her to the edge of the bed. She drops to her knees, begins kissing sucking stroking Kathy's breasts. Kathy shivers, wonders when the clamps will come, but cannot resist that devouring mouth. She is almost coming *please fuck me please fuck me* and closes her eyes – and there, she feels it, not on her breasts, no, but that vicious bite on her clit. Kathy's eyes snap open to Ruby smirking, she wants to slap her, to strike her but *tug* and she is up, a shock that must be on her face because Ruby is laughing *tug tug* and she follows *tug* up *tug* down, she's a marionette on a string. "I could parade you in the hall like this," Ruby chuckles. *Tug tug.*

Kathy swallows. *Would she dare? Would she dare?*

"Jules!" Jules appears at the door. Ruby *tug tug* smiles. "Take her for a ride." At the door, "Oh." Kathy turns for a reprieve *this can't be happening to me* but Ruby takes out her lipstick, writes something on Kathy's back.

"What's that?"

Ruby turns her back to the mirror. Written neatly are the words "Fuck Virgin." Kathy is mortified. Ruby explains, "They can eat you, but they can't make you come. And no," Ruby's fingers pump the air, "penetration. Jules will make sure of that."

"Please –" Kathy rushes forward but the chain bites at her clit.

Jules tug tugs her out of the room, into the hallway. Women passing, smile at the slickness shining between Kathy's thighs. Kathy leans against the banister, looks over the rail, sees a crowd of women, does not want to go down the stairs. She leans forward and feels a kiss, a tongue between her cunt lips, starts, but *tug* Jules pulling the chain through the posts, pins her to the rail, Jules' tongue trilling against her, *plop plop plop* play of frothing wetness, Jules' moan humming into her, a slap and teeth against her ass, another tug, her laughing sigh. "I could keep you spread out like this, for every woman. But maybe we should go down into the hall."

Kathy tries to look dignified, walking down the stairs, but every so often Jules gives her a tug and she cries out, nearly stumbles. Jules vanishes in the crowd ahead of her, but still the chain. In the crush of bodies, again the hands are everywhere, two mouths on her tits, nails stroking belly, and god, light tease caress as pussy juice squeezes out of her, a woman kisses her full on the mouth, places Kathy's hand down there, in her own honeyed pot, sweet offerings but *tug tug* she must follow, down the hall.

The room is dark, lit by the dim light of long thick candles. Kathy can barely put one foot in front of the other as Jules catches her, lays her on a table, but her legs float, toes suckled, so many mouths she struggles but always falls, drips back into her pussy her sobs of *fuck me fuck me* her throat abraded, pushed back.

The clamp is off but too sore too sore she shrieks as the air brushes her. She blinks, blinks, sees the mirrors, the rack at her side, cuntshiver, she can't take this any more, can't fuck, can barely stand. She hears a titter in the audience and knows. Ruby steps to the platform/bed, wheels the rack in front of her. She descends on Kathy's hips, opening her legs, pinning her down. Kathy sees this in the mirror, her red puffy torment, Ruby's slow even smile. Ruby whispers, "Did anyone touch you?"

A moment's panic as Kathy thinks of Ruby's rules. "Y-yes."

Ruby's hand dipping into the water, droplets plip plip on lips, clit, and Kathy thrashes *too much* the clamp still biting even though it's gone. Kathy's gasping breath, she sees the mirror and Ruby holds her firm, she sees Ruby's tongue flicker, in the eternity before she's there. Kathy arches, the cries torn out of her, but Ruby, on for the ride, buries herself in Kathy's burrow, holds on for dear life as Kathy tries to shake her, spasms rolling as Kathy collapses shameless mindless need her *RubyRubyRuby* chanting from her lips, Kathy almost lost now, thinks she can take anything, her body blasted beyond her senses, lies back, breathes, lets her muscles go.

Hot. Searing hot. Ruby drips hot wax on her breasts.

And Kathy's whole body bucks, almost throwing her, Kathy kicking, arms swinging, a screeching, keening wail. Ruby strokes her, the butt of the candle plunging into her pussy, deeper deeper slippery wax bites along furrows, in cunt depths, deeper, until she cannot bear it, almost there but Ruby pulls, pulls the stick of of her, lights the bottom, a sizzle as cunt juice vaporizes, the candle burning at both ends now.

Ruby sits, panting. Her eyes smart from her sweat. Kathy cannot sit, cannot even cry. Her arm up, no control, as she tries to hit Ruby, but it falls, barely a caress. Ruby holds her, rocks, feels the tears, kisses them away. "Babybabybaby," she croons, "I haven't really fucked you yet."

♀

Kathy dreams of flight. She's being chased down and down the spiral stairs, hand sliding on the banister, through the labyrinth of corridors, out the door, her robe twisting around her legs as she runs down the hill, jumps stones across a river, but she falls, waist deep, the current flings her back. She claws her way up the bank, can hear them behind her, their heavy footfalls, panting breath, she flees into the darkening woods but the path grows narrower the deeper she goes until it stops altogether. She's surrounded by tall thick blackberry bushes, tangled vines. Kathy's long hair catches in the nettles, she's on a path with no exit. She hears a crash behind her, she can see the sky so far away. She spies a small break in the thicket, a breach by the ground, a rabbit hole perhaps. She pushes her arms through, then her chest, feels the pricks and scratches of the sharp nasty thorns, and pulls – but the hole contracts, hips too wide and she is frantic now, kicking, she can hear them, the wolves at the door, feel the heavy puffs of their exertion, the loll of tongues against jagged teeth. She's Little Red riding without the hood, a Beauty lanced into dreamless sleep. She feels them close, her robe in shreds, they're smashing through the bushes, trampling the fruit. Kathy feels the earth tremor – and they're there, prey in sight, and howl, a cry of triumph.

Kathy jolts from her nightmare. She is in the Red Room, face down on the bed. She knows this place. How many times has she woken here, her body floating on these satiny sheets. She feels a slow burn on her backside, remembers the ice, the clamps, and Ruby, and burrows into her pillow. She no longer has any tears, her body opened, exposed in the auditorium, that burning shame, such public desire. She shakes away the memory. Sighs. She can feel the wind playing havoc with the caressing sheets, pleasure of lying, a body at rest. It seems she has always been in this room, but thinks of the truck, her father's house, school that she dreads and despises. Her other life. But soon, she'll be eighteen, out of school, then no one can tell her what to do.

She turns her face, sees Ruby in the mirror, between her parted legs, a velvet mitten on her hand, stroking ass dip thighs. "Ruby," she chokes, but doesn't fight it, feels herself melting, the slickness does not lie. Ruby lifts hips high, mouth sinking, sucking to the pink shell of her cunt, rubbing her cheeks to peachy fuzz, a circle and back, descending and back. Kathy feels the coils tightening deeper than her cunt, she wants Ruby in there, how the ache has never left, never retreated, but spirals inwards, clenching, unclenching. She's got to fuck her now, now or never, Kathy can't pull away. Her arms are shaking as Ruby turns her over, kisses her, pulls back her hair.

"The next time you come," Ruby whispers, "I want to be inside you."

Kathy licks her lips, needs to say it, trips over the words. "Ruby, I want to fuck you."

Ruby laughs. "You want to flip me? Not yet, Kathy." She nuzzles closer, "But later I want you to. I want you to enjoy this."

"When I touch you, something happens to me, it becomes bigger, it. . . ."

"Turns you on."

Kathy reddens.

"The first time I saw you, I wanted to spread your legs and dive inside. But you were so scared. I didn't want to hurt you and I didn't want to rush. I want you to savour this, every moment, this sensation."

"It's just . . . I've waited so long."

Ruby smiles. "In some ways I envy you."

Kathy blinks, swallows.

"All this," Ruby's hand strokes Kathy's belly, "is new."

Kathy sits up on her elbows. "How was your first time?"

"Mmm. Embarrassing. For a long time I didn't know what I wanted, or what to do, really. And she was, well, ambivalent about things. We'd been drinking, out swimming in the river. It'd been so hot but diving into that water, it was like you'd left everything behind, that anything could happen. It's hard to explain. Something to do with being drunk and seventeen. I'd wanted her so bad, for such a long time, and I couldn't figure it out. At least until that night. She couldn't swim very well, and I was holding her from behind, saying look at the minnows, the little fishes. But it was my hand, my fingers teasing her along her thighs, between her lips. I'd dive and just stare at her, those breasts, stroke her as I was helping her to float. I remember her at the dock, she was pulling herself up and for a moment she hung there, her pussy, that sweet ass, and I just grabbed her, rammed my tongue inside, god, I ate her forever, and that taste, thick, like syrup on the tongue. I'd never seen anyone, not like that, not before. I can still remember her smell and that feeling, when she turned around and opened her legs, or better yet, when she threw her hips at me, her hands in my hair, that little cry she gave when she came. Afterwards, she said she couldn't remember."

Kathy looks down. "Last year I kissed a girl. Or she kissed me. We'd just beaten Lancaster seven to one. Field hockey. I thought it meant something else. The kiss, I mean. In the bus, after the game, I touched her. I was expelled and no one ever talked to me after that."

"Oh, Kathy."

Her voice almost breaking, "I thought that maybe she wanted me."

"If it means anything, I want you."

Kathy, wistful, "I bet you say that to all the girls."

Ruby laughs, traces her lips, leans in to kiss her, then changes her mind. "Kathy." She takes Kathy's hand, places it between her own parted legs. "Did you touch her here?"

"No."

"Or here?" Ruby offering, places Kathy's other hand on her breast.

Fullness, the stiff nipple and ring of areola, the flush of Ruby's chest, shallowness of breath. Kathy takes Ruby into her mouth, wants to swallow, she sucks and pinches, fingers twist as her other fingers flutter and swim. Ruby sighs, spreads herself wide. Kathy wants to see her, almost cries at the gift, sinks down to the open petals, the rising bud, longs to taste her, but gazes. Kathy watches her fingers enter, Ruby's cunt taking her in, the thrust and retreat, thrust and retreat, fingers gliding into the wet. And Ruby's face, the silent *oh* as Kathy opens her, how she gives and gives, how generously she takes. Ruby's hips rising, moving with the rhythm, into her into her and Kathy pops out, Ruby shuddering against the loss. Kathy sees the sweat glowing on Ruby's chest, the heaviness in her eyes. So close, so close. She brings her hand up to smell her, sucks her fingers as Ruby stares. Slowly Kathy descends, biting, nibbling, to those open thighs, Kathy gazing into those lips, a flick before she plunges inside, Ruby's hips rolling with her, hands in her hair, tongue fuck fuck fucking her, stroke nibbling roll and swirl, unfurling those folds, suck slurping burrowing deep, as Ruby on the edge, one finger wriggling, two thrusting, a third, pushing her orgasm up and over, cunt grip rippling through, Ruby's cries as it shakes her, soaring to her release.

Ruby falls back on the bed, a sense of languor trickling through her limbs. She stretches and closes her eyes. Kathy gazes, feels recklessness, feels greedy, then slowly creeping, feels deliciously smug. She slinks down to Ruby's pussy and begins suckling, tongue exploring those hidden folds. Kathy can taste the fresh cunt juice dripping over chin, wants to soak in more. Her mouth wanders over Ruby's mons, a taunting, lighter torment. Ruby's hips shift, tries to catch her, but how quickly she darts and flies. Kathy lifts her head. She feels her strength and wants to flaunt it, wants to hear Ruby beg. Ruby opens her eyes. Kathy sits, hips grinding over Ruby's belly, smears her wetness all over, raises herself so Ruby can see the dampened bush, unveiling her clitoris. Ruby tries to roll her off, but Kathy pins her. She straddles her cunt over Ruby's face, feels sure of herself, on top, but too soon, the tongue, silky, languid tongue, not the shooting dart so expected, but slow, that Kathy presses down, a trap as Ruby grabs her, clit sucksucksucking cuntfest fuck breaking down as *please yes* rider ridden from the bottom up and Kathy comes, she's thrown.

Ruby eases her down, she is shaking, limbs rubbery. Ruby is bemused and smiling. She parts Kathy's legs, gestures to the mirror at the foot of the bed, and Kathy sees herself laid bare. "Look. You're so beautiful." Ruby slips a finger inside, and Kathy, so close from coming, clutches at it, but slow slow Ruby stokes her, forces a different rhythm. Kathy stares at the mirror, sees Ruby inside her. Strong arms pin her down. Ruby slips out and Kathy almost cries. With two fingers Ruby caresses the mons, two fingers lingering along the lips, and snap – a pinch of clit. Kathy screams, slaps her thighs together. But Ruby whispers, works them open, a soothing tongue, hands cupping ass, so sweet. She moves and the mirror is there again, her finger dipping in and out, then two, two in two out two in. A *pleaseplease* from Kathy, as she feels the fullness stretching the tightness of her cunt, so good, slipping deeper *please more* a contracting edge of pain. Ruby feels this, she reaches for the rack beside her, the bowl of lube, three fingers slipping in, Kathy's arching back at this fullness, sobbing *Ruby please* as Ruby's arm *pump* fucks her in staccato thrusts *pleasegod* and Kathy can't hold and *pump pump pump* she comes screaming, shouting, a curse and a roar.

Kathy curls up on herself as Ruby holds her. "Sorry," she murmurs, and swallows.

"Sorry? For what?"

"Coming too soon."

Ruby smiles. "Why too soon?"

"I wanted . . . your hand . . . all inside me."

Ruby laughs. "You want everything yesterday," and kisses her. "Rest. And then we'll see what we can do."

Kathy sleeps in the Red Room. And when she wakes, Ruby will be waiting.

♀

X closes the book, gazes at Y, asleep in the comforters. X sighs. But tomorrow . . . and there are always other stories. She looks so beautiful, X realizes, and no writer could ever capture that. And tomorrow, tomorrow X will tell her.

Quixotic

The Island of

JIANI

An island of women. A paradise, perhaps, but not for her.

The moon was low, sparkling above the waters. Across the inlet Miru could see the tangled groves, and far beyond, the mountains of swaying bamboo. The warm surf splashed at her feet, pulling the sand from her heels. Water sprites, the villagers had whispered, the demon in the mountains.

The villagers told tales, but what did they know of the island? Stone city walls, a sheltered port, not the wild hills and wind–swept beaches, not the waterfalls, the gushing springs, the heavy boughs laden with fruit, not the rolling meadows with their tickling grasses, nor the lazy shallows of the river.

The sea, so calm.

Miru stripped off her dress and dove into the waves. Legs kicking, arms at full reach, slipping through currents, stroking with tide. She loved the swirls and eddies, flux and flow against her limbs. The water held her, buoyant, surrounding her, she could feel its resistance, its pull, the strength of surge, the caress of release. She swam, engulfed, enfolded, sailing motion, skimming ride.

To the beach now, panting, she fell against the shore. Exhausted, she slept.

Earthly Delights

And dreamt.

And woke with a start, as if not alone. Spinning earth, rolling sky.

The tide had risen, the surf lapping between her legs, the sun peering over the horizon.

But, she thought, someone, something had touched her there, a finger's caress. She scanned up and down the beach. No one.

She stared between her legs, the light falling on those fragrant curls. Those lips, swollen with another wetness, thick and salty sweet.

She shivered and rose, legs shaking.

No. No. Her imagination.

The air, heavy against her skin, and distantly, the cry of cicadas through the groves of green, green bamboo.

No.

Miru walked through the lowland rice fields, her feet sinking, the clutch of mud between her toes, the tender rice seedlings grazing her legs, sauntered to the thick maze of bushes, in the crook of the rising hills. She plucked the red ripeness, prickle berries, a burst of sweetness in her mouth.

The sun, higher now, the island, lushly green.

Still the lingering slickness between her thighs.

The branches caught at her naked reach, scratching, jagged

thorns, the leaves spilling droplets from the night's rain.

She bent to gather the plumpest berries, deep in the entangling vines. Stretching, she felt it, a kiss, the lightest breeze between her pussy lips – then a plunging tongue.

She screamed, her hand slapping down over her vulva, and turned.

No one. Stillness in the thick of the bush.

Her eyes darted, searching through the leaves.

She ran, ran through the meadow, the long grasses whipping her calves, the tall wheat stalks brushing her thighs, ran to the river, the calm lazy shallows, and stopped at a clear, still pool.

Miru stood at the pool's edge and squatted. In the reflection, she examined her lips, those folds. Wet. Hesitant, she slid a finger inside and felt the thrill of entering herself. She blushed. Her own imagination. What else could it be? She remembered the time she fell asleep in the fields, and come morning, the dew drops had gathered in the curls of her pussy hair, slid down between her lips and she awakened to a caress. Yes, that's what it was. Or under the waterfall, she had stood, eyes closed, washing away the heat, water beating, sluicing through her legs, she felt hands gripping her breasts, but no, an aimless gust of wind.

Yes, she told herself, quelling her fears. Yes.

The hot sun, the sweetness of berries, her uneasy night on the shore.

Miru remembered, once, in the heat of the afternoon, she and Jiani were napping on the thatch. They lay naked, dozing, back to back. But restless, she turned, flipped, her head near Jiani's feet. She opened her eyes and saw the moistness between Jiani's thighs, that slick treasure. As if in sleep, her arms curled around her friend, and her face pressed down. How long had she breathed on that tender furrow? Her fingers reaching up, stroking Jiani's mound, her tongue lapping Jiani's saltiness.

The temple bell rang and they had woken. They both had had the strangest dream.

And she remembered on the trek to the mountain. They had gone to see the snow monkeys bathing in the hot volcanic waters. Jiani had been climbing above her. She had looked up, gazed upon that slickness once more. The rock had been uneven, and Jiani tumbled. Catching her, Miru's hand had slipped between Jiani's thighs, a finger lodging within. Miru held her, to calm her, she told herself, her finger firmly inside, Jiani's breath, so close, so shaken from the fall.

She shook off her memories. Jiani was now in the priestess's house.

She stood, looked up the hill, and began walking.

At the crest of the hill stood an old gnarled pine tree, branches low, spreading. Here she could sleep in the crook of the lowest bough. Miru scampered up the rough bark, where, in her favourite spot, a gash had opened and the wood was smooth but for one tiny knot. Above, the leaves floated green, a cooling canopy. She slept.

Again she dreamt.

And when she woke, her cunt, swollen, wet, as if someone had been stroking her.

She sat up, straddling her branch.

No no no. Her imagination. The air, so humid, clung.

But why?

She thought of the temple, of how Jiani had spilled a rice bowl on her lap during the festival feast. Naked, her body was covered with stickiness and the priestess had punished Jiani in front of everyone by licking off every bit.

But the small grains, clinging inside her cunt.

The priestess had taken her to the table, spread her open, eaten the tender morsels out, her tongue exploring every fold, every crevice, swallowing, sucking, Jiani, those tears, but she had seen it, the priestess's finger, below, dipping into Jiani's asshole, a wetness, not just from the priestess's mouth.

Jiani in the priestess's house.

Jealous, yes – of her friend, or the priestess?

Straddled on the branch, she was rocking, unknowingly, the movement a comfort, a solace.

But Miru felt it, the tiny knob, the knot on smooth, glistening wood. She gave herself to the motion, eyes closed, the gash on the tree, so much like a mouth, rubbing, rubbing, lips, she could feel it, her juices, streaming, her hips riding faster faster, her rhythm peaking – a tongue slicing into her – and she screamed, stumbled off her mount – she knew it was there, she'd been sitting on it, sinking, a mouth, devouring, feasting, and her cunt was burning.

She stared at the tree, the branch.

No tongue. No lips. No mouth.

Miru glared over the valley, enraged, and screamed her fury.

Distantly, she heard the temple bell.

She ran down the hill, to the valley, into the temple, back into the recesses of the great hall, and silently, into the sanctum.

The priestess was there, and before her, on the altar, naked and spread wide, Jiani.

"Promise me," Jiani whispered, "this time. This time she will be mine."

The priestess nodded. "She will be yours."

The priestess poured her libation between Jiani's legs. A moan from Jiani, rocking hips, spreading thighs. From the table the priestess took a pliant stick, twisted into a v-shaped form. A rippled double dildo. "Let this be your last gift to me," the priestess smiled, and slowly, teasingly slid the stick into Jiani's opening.

Jiani's body arched, a gasp.

The priestess pulled out the wet end and inserted this into her own vagina. With bindings, she strapped it snugly in.

"Begin," the priestess commanded.

In a low whisper, Jiani began her prayer.

"Goddess, give her back to me, let the winds of the island entice her, let the waters persuade, let the trees and the hills caress and cajole her, take my offering."

The priestess lay over her, the tip of the stick stroking Jiani's lips. She kissed Jiani's breasts, suckling, and guided the shaft into her.

In the shadows of the sanctum, Miru could feel (or imagine?) the shaft entering, a deep thrust inside her as the priestess dove, Jiani's cry, Miru's own pleasure as the priestess, hips bucking, plunged, reckless, Miru's own need as the priestess fucked Jiani, fucked *her*, Miru's cunt muscles pummeled, legs giving way, a brutal wrenching orgasm, as the priestess slammed into her, her Jiani.

Miru staggered to the altar, pulled the priestess off, the dildo out. Jiani looked up through tears. Miru brushed back Jiani's long entangled hair. Smiled down and wept. Her fingers were inside Jiani, she would not let her go, she took her to the waterfall, to the oak tree, to the shore, she fucked her fiercely, for all the days of torment, her restless nights, she fucked her, as Jiani had, even in her dreams.

♀

But Miru, has she imagined this, this torment, this desire? The island's whisper, the sea tide's foam. Only the priestess, smiling, can say.

The Tale of the Moon Woman

There was a young woman who wished to be fucked by the moon. She would lie in the tide, the moonlight gleaming on her skin, legs open. But the moon, so distant, would not accept her offer. The villagers shook their heads. What could be done?

Now this woman had an admirer who was determined to possess her, in the worst possible way. This admirer was something of a trickster. With a pearl harvester's net in hand she would roam the beaches, asking young women if they had seen her lost pearl, and spying this jewel clinging in the folds of the woman's legs, she would lie them down and suck to her heart's content.

Now the admirer knew that the answer to the moon woman's quest lay with the priestess, who was the wisest woman on the isle. So the admirer put away her trappings and net, and into the temple she went. She poured her libation and prayed. The priestess appeared and placed in the admirer's hands a gleaming white dildo cut from the youngest jade. The admirer was confused.

If you look at it head on, it looks like the moon, explained the priestess, now suck out my pearl. If you fuck me with it, I'll throw in the harness for free.

And so the admirer left the temple with the moon stick, the juices of the priestess dripping down her chin, the harness in hand.

On that moonless night the admirer approached the moon woman, who lay on the shore.

I have your heart's desire, she cried out, and she pulled out the jade stick, careful that the moon woman saw it head on.

The moon woman gasped, stepped forward. But the admirer cautioned, not so fast, lie down, you'll need help with this, the moon's not a trifling thing. And close your eyes, it's sacred, not for mortal eyes.

The moon woman closed her eyes. The admirer strapped on the jade stick and rode her with the tide. She fucked her to her heart's content, lifting her hips, slamming inside.

Every night the moon woman waited and every night the admirer appeared, moon stick in hand.

On the night of the next full moon the admirer met the moon woman on the beach. The moon woman was desolate.

Why so sad? the admirer asked.

The moon woman pointed at the sky, at the full shining moon. She has forsaken me.

No, said the admirer, and she guided the moon woman's hand to the moon stick nestled in the harness.

But how? asked the moon woman.

The moon grows back, the admirer explained, pressing the moon woman down.

But the light of the moon –

Has rubbed off in your pussy, the admirer continued.

Then I'll have the moon inside me forever.

Forever, replied the admirer as she slid the stick inside her and she fucked her till she cried.

♀

Later, when the admirer slipped into the temple to pay homage to the wise woman, she saw the moon woman suckling at the priestess's clit. The priestess smoothed back the moon woman's hair and smiling, asked, Was it worth the wait, this performance, your lies, all this for a trickster, a pearl-sucking rogue?

Ah, she hasn't fucked you.

Ah, my dear, she has.

YUKI ONNA

There was a legend on the island of earthly delights that when the north wind blew in the eleventh month, the Yuki Onna would return to the high mountain. Now the Yuki Onna was a snow demon who would suck the life out of any living creature that came across her path. Every year the miners who worked the mountain ridge waited in terror for the sign.

That year the north wind blasted deadly cold on the very first day of the eleventh month.

The miners fled.

Now in the village there lived a thoughtful young woman named Miyako. She had heard of the legend of the Yuki Onna and of the miners' flight, so she decided to go up to the peak to investigate this phenomenon. All alone she trekked up the narrow path and settled into a crude shack with her provisions. She lit her lamp and stoked the fire and waited for the coming storm.

The wind howled fiercely, rattled the windows, pounded on the door, but Miyako was not shaken. She read her books and sipped her tea. At last she decided to go to bed. She had slipped into her robe and turned down the covers when the door slammed open. The wind blew out the fire and knocked over the lamp, but still the young woman could see her: the Yuki Onna sliding into the cabin.

She slid as if on sheets of ice, her breath a crystalline mist. Her lips were blue and her hair long and black, and she wore a kimono that sparkled like frost, trailing far behind her.

The young woman stared. So it was true. The Yuki Onna was beautiful but cold, deadly cold. How must it be, Miyako thought, to spend your days in this wintry embrace. Outside the wind howled and shrieked. How terrible to be alone and immortal.

Miyako picked up her lamp. "Don't be afraid," she said.

The Yuki Onna stopped in her tracks. What impertinence! She glided forward. "I could have spared you for your beauty, but no, I will take your life."

Miyako, who had started the fire blazing again, turned to the Yuki Onna. "Will you suck out my breath? Freeze the blood in my veins?" Miyako pulled off her robe, "Or turn my heart to ice?" She stood naked in front of the Yuki Onna, the warm lamp light shimmering across her belly. The Yuki Onna stared, disbelieving. Miyako took the Yuki Onna's hand. "Your hands are cold, let me warm them for you," and saying this, she placed one of the Yuki Onna's hands on her breast, the other she nestled between her thighs.

The Yuki Onna stood confounded; there was no fear, no terror, only living warmth, the silkiness between thighs, the plumpness of breast. She gazed at the dark ring of areola, the pert nipples, the muscles along the collarbone, the slender nape of neck. How dare she! the Yuki Onna thought, but her hand, tickled by her pubic hair, and so close to Miyako's opening, began to stroke. I will suck the life out of her, the Yuki Onna decided, but the young woman had already stepped forward and began kissing the Yuki Onna's lips.

Soft, so soft, living breathing flesh, the edge of her teeth and a darting, mischievous tongue. A kiss so deep that the Yuki Onna felt herself stirring in her secret depths. Tiny, goading nibbles along her chin, rough teeth marks on her neck, and stinging bites on her shoulder. And hands, exploring the folds of her kimono from silk to skin, a brush on the small of her back. The kimono slipped off her shoulder, to the floor.

The young woman gazed at the Yuki Onna. A pink flush had appeared in her cheeks, a glimmer in those dark eyes. The Yuki Onna kissed her again, wanting to stoke, to feel the heat beneath her hands.

Slowly, the Yuki Onna was melting with desire. She wanted to feel with all of her senses, after all her years in the cold.

The Yuki Onna pushed the young woman onto the narrow bed. She climbed on top of her, felt the length of her body against her own, belly against belly, thighs against thighs, and hands flitting everywhere, a hunger of touch. The Yuki Onna turned Miyako over, rubbed deep into her back, into the broad expanse of shoulders, down to strong thighs, the tickle behind her knees. The Yuki Onna pressed her hips against Miyako's ass, her breasts crushed against Miyako's back, and rocking, felt deliciously alive. She could feel the heat from the young woman's cunt, the wetness within her folds. The Yuki Onna's hand snaked down. . . .

But Miyako turned. "No." She smiled and stepped out of the narrow bed.

She stacked the pillows and pushed the Yuki Onna back and knelt in front of her. Gently she nudged open the Yuki Onna's legs and smiled when she saw her glistening prize. Oh, beautiful sight! Damp curls, and cunt so wet! She stared, so tempted.

But not yet.

Miyako began with the Yuki Onna's slender foot, the tender arch, licking those lovely toes. Her mouth working up to the fragile ankles, the thick calves, the strong thighs, but she stopped when the Yuki Onna's pubic hair tickled her nose. Her hands slid around, back, down to cup the Yuki Onna's ass, and pulled her closer.

Breasts, her mouth taking in nipples as her own grazed the Yuki Onna's belly, suckling play, lips kissing up to mouth, tongue and tongue swirling, as the young woman's fingers began caressing the damp mound.

The Yuki Onna moaned, hips pitching forward.

Miyako sat back, watched as the Yuki Onna writhed under her touches, wetness coming quicker now, cunt muscles twitching. She gazed as the Yuki Onna spread her legs wider, exposing those inner folds, her inflamed clitoris, that hidden orifice, slick with nectar.

Beautiful, Miyako gazed. Beautiful.

She leaned in, smelled the heavy fragrance, breathed on those parted lips. Slowly, ever so slowly, her tongue began a flickering dance, exploring her crevices, outer lips, the groove between her thighs. Inch by inch, so very slowly, tasting, teasing, finally burrowing into her hole, the fuck of tongue, slithering into the Yuki Onna like an electric flash.

Again the young woman leaned back to gaze upon her feast. Smiling, she raised the Yuki Onna's leg over her shoulder and slid a finger into her vagina.

Fullness, different from that naughty tongue, a firm stroke against her vaginal walls, deeper, a curling motion. Sliding in and out, the Yuki Onna jerked with every thrust. Her groans were guttural now, deep, as the young woman's finger fucked them out of her. Two fingers and Miyako's mouth descended, suckling the clit as she rocked her insides, faster, lapping to her own rhythm of pleasure.

Miyako felt her fingers pushed out, the cunt ripples under her tongue. She plunged in deeper, thrust faster, sucked harder, riding out the spasms until the Yuki Onna could give her no more.

♀

Inside the shack, as the winds howled outside, the Yuki Onna curled around Miyako.

"I will spare you, but promise me that you will never tell another living soul about this night, for if you do I must come and take your soul."

The young woman promised and with that, the Yuki Onna disappeared without a trace.

♀

The following spring, as Miyako was watching the fireflies by the river, she saw a figure walking along the wooden bridge. The woman looked familiar somehow. They began walking side by side and Miyako became entranced by the woman's laughter, her stories of the fate of the stars, and why the mists cling to the river. As they walked to Miyako's house, she didn't notice how the woman's feet never touched the ground.

Her name was Fuyu. As it was dark, and Fuyu was far from her mountain home, Miyako offered her a place for the night.

That night Miyako woke, robe open, Fuyu kneeling between her open legs, a lamp by her side.

"Yuki Onna," Miyako gasped.

The Yuki Onna's breath floated, crystalline, in the air. She snapped back the trailing sleeves of her kimono, and slowly straddled Miyako. "Choose," she whispered. "Choose between immortality, or these transient pleasures. My gift, for you have not broken my trust."

Miyako's hand slipped through the Yuki Onna's kimono, holding the seat of her weakness, her power.

"Choose?" Miyako replied. "Between one or the other? What godhead could you offer me? What future could you divine?" Miyako's fingers, tracing the edges of the Yuki Onna's cunt, so close and yet so far. "Choose? I choose both." And saying this, Miyako slid into the Yuki Onna, filling her, fucking her, timeless and forever.

On an isle not far from the Island of Earthly Delights, there lived a white magician and his daughter. Now the magician ruled this land. He had arrived in tall black ships, conquered the inhabitants, and built his magnificent castle of stone. But the nights were cold in his palace and his daughter was all alone. (The magician did not care for the inhabitants of the isle, for he was a civilized man.) One day the magician called to his daughter and told her he was going away for seven weeks. The Queen of the distant Imperium had summoned him. He told her that she could have the run of the castle but she must never go into the dungeon – there, the beast of the island was imprisoned and it was a calamity to set eyes upon it.

"Miranda, it will devour you and tear your limbs asunder and your soul will be perpetually damned," her father whispered, stroking his long grey beard. The daughter nodded dutifully. Reassured, the magician went on his way.

As she saw his ship slip over the horizon, Miranda skipped through the vast halls of her prison. From her window in the clouds, she could see the bustling life of the city below, hear the cries of the vendors, the *hanabi* bursting in the distance. How she longed to join the throngs that her father detested, to move among life. Asiatics, he called them, with a sneer, for he was a

Beast

rational man, a scientific man, his magics were of pure reason. But below, he only saw the masses, his own constructions of an other, incomprehensible life.

Miranda sighed, looked to the distant mountain range. She had never traveled and her father had been her only companion for as long as she could remember. She was a stranger in this land her father ruled, a stranger in every land. Even this castle was not her home, and Miranda desperately wanted a home. She sat in the turret, spinning her own tales of full, exciting lives.

Miranda turned, listened.

A roar. No. A low and keening moan. From the dungeon.

The daughter ran down the stairwell, her father's exhortation ringing in her ears.

But that moan. Not monstrous, not horrifying. Just lonely, painfully so.

She paused at the dungeon door.

What harm is there in a look? she thought. Miranda stooped and peered through the keyhole. The room was dark and she could not see even the faintest shift nor shadow.

A voice, rasping and low, came from the depths of the chamber. "Who are you? Why do you come, peering through the keyhole. Are you afraid? Of me, or of the dark?"

Miranda froze, terrified. The voice of the beast. But she had not seen it.

"I am not afraid of you!" Miranda cried, a little too shrill, even as her voice bounced off the dank walls of the chamber.

The beast spoke slowly, as if unaccustomed to the workings of its tongue. "Not afraid. That is good. Speak to me in this darkness, so I may know that I am not alone."

Miranda, surprised, asked, "Are you lonely?"

"Yes."

"Why are you locked up? Why can't I see you?"

The beast did not reply.

"What are you?"

The beast whispered, "Look up."

Miranda looked up. Far, far above she could see a hole in the ceiling of the castle, and beyond, the darkness and glittering stars.

"Do you see them?"

"Yes."

"I have not seen stars, oh, for such a long time, I can no longer imagine them. Did I dream them, dream light, dream beauty? When I was little, I was told that it was the stars that held up the canopy of the night, and if they fell, the world would be crushed by darkness. Perhaps it has come true."

"What are you?"

Caliban reads in the first tower of the third wing. Around her form the corridors of a labyrinth, the shelves a barricade in luminescent glow. As she studies the pages before her, the scratch of parchment, the unfolding lies, she can feel the dust on her fingertips, the palimpsest lives. Careless, she brushes back her long black hair. She holds such words as ontological on her tongue, slips between onomatopoeia and oxymoron. She is not aware of the weight of leaves pressing upon leaves, the abyss between the lines. Caliban thinks of history as once upon a time. She spreads the map, Novae Insvlae, Munster, c. 1540, unscrolling the world before her, the regions of emptiness, headless men,

The beast sighed. "Shall I tell you a story?"

"Yes."

"Then open the door."

Miranda hesitated. "I cannot. My father says you would devour me and tear my limbs asunder and my soul would be perpetually damned."

"Father?" the beast groaned. "Father?" A terrible cry came from the depths of the darkness, a wild, heartbreaking sorrow. Miranda placed her hands over her ears and ran and ran, but she could still feel the echoes ringing in the empty chambers of the tower. She flung herself into bed and cried herself to sleep.

♀

She woke as the light fell through her windows, the prism's dance of a thousand colours, as her crystals spun in the wind. I live in a fairy tale, she thought, a beauty still sleeping in her father's castle. No, this, this will not do.

She ran down to the dungeon and flung opened the door, her lamp casting a small pool of light, a knife clutched in her hand.

At first sight, the daughter started: monstrous indeed, the beast had the head of a bull. It was swarthed in ragged pelts and she could smell its foulness even from the door. She could see the blood, thickened and dried, where manacles had cut into flesh, the scars

---

and raging beasts. The world opens to Pythagoras and his spheres, the lines of Euclid, the points of the Nile. Within walls, between windows of pebbled glass, Caliban waits, tracing a cartography of time. Caliban waits, between dead-end partitions, the annex, an alcove, a sheaf of lives. And there she is, between Canibali and Regio Gigantum. She traces a line from Asia Noviter Delineata, Blaeu, 1662. From Ia Pan to the space between giants and cannibals. She laughs. She knows these maps are fictions.

Caliban walks home in the rain. Above her the street lamps glow, misty orbs that float and dance. Could the heavens be so close, so clear? Caliban

from lashes across its shoulders, and it looked so pitifully thin. But the beast still looked fearsome, its eyes gazed dead, lolled forward.

Miranda stepped forward. Something was not right, its head –

The lamp dipped.

The beast howled at the light searing its eyes, jerked in its chains and knocked the lamp from Miranda's hand. A shatter of glass and Miranda screamed, scuttling into the corner. But still the locks, the beast's raw fury. Miranda shook, as the beast began smashing its head against the dungeon wall. That awful sound of flesh striking stone. Chains clanking, scraping against the wall, the pitch of a body flung against their length. Such harrowing thrashing, such fathomless grief. Miranda backed away. Pity and terror spun in her brain.

Miranda fled.

♀

Miranda paced the halls. She had not eaten, had not slept, her mind racing around the mystery of the monster below. She had read of minotaurs in mazes, but this one was caged, devoid of light, of company. The beast was chained, and she, Miranda, was no coward.

She crept down the stone staircase. Besides, she thought, the beast must be hungry.

---

does not care, sips *ocha* and nibbles on *sembei*. She slips into a warm bed of leaves, wriggling her toes in delight. She sleeps. And dreams of minotaurs in mazes.

♀

Caliban reads in the second tower of the fifth wing. Here the mirrors shine into infinity, reflections of stone, refractions of glass. On the table, the unspiraling world. Caliban peers into India Extra Gangem, the void beyond the end of the word. She thinks of the legends of Alexander, the *Iliad*, and of Homer, a father

From the kitchen she took sweet meats and bread, and from the table, a pitcher of water.

Wrapping a gauze scarf around her lamp, she crept down the stairway with her provisions to the dungeon hall. The scarf will shield its eyes, Miranda thought, for she realized that to a creature of darkness such illumination was painful.

She opened the door.

The beast had not moved. The beast with the bull's head, and cold, dead, unblinking eyes.

She saw the horns, the manacles, the bloodied flesh.

She crept closer.

As she reached out and stroked the appalling horns, the mask tumbled off. Beneath, a woman, not unlike herself, but black, black hair, and dark eyes, skin so terribly abraded. Miranda shifted, something, something monstrous must be here – why else the lashes and this brutal captivity?

The beast blinked slowly, exhausted.

Gently, Miranda pressed the pitcher to the beast's cracked and bleeding lips, and slowly dribbled the liquid into the beast's mouth, stroking her throat, helping her swallow. The beast drank, listless. Miranda picked up the knife, and began picking at the manacles. The locks were rusted and the springs in the clasp broke easily.

---

of tales. She flips back her hair, wine–dark. Her heart is not with the warriors, but with the women: Andromach, Hecuba, Cressida, and Cassandra, their narratives of exile, slavery, madness, and death. Caliban thinks of Medea, of her journey across the seas. She looks in the mirror but has no children to kill, merely an image reflected a thousandfold. On the maps she marks the places of her birth, her mouth holds the name, swallowing. Even her tongue is foreign to her lips. Between the points of her fingers there is a journey of a thousand and one days. She traces the path of the chariot, Medea's getaway. She frowns. She knows these maps are riddles.

The beast fell forward.

Miranda thought, this is a monster? So terribly thin and helpless. She carried the beast up the stairs, into her chamber. There, Miranda tore away the bedraggled pelts and bathed her in warm, scented waters. She brushed away the encrusted blood, soothed the wounds, held her floating in the marbled pool. She fed her bread dipped in milk, caressed her face, crushed berries and spooned them through barely parted lips. When Miranda carried her to the silken bed, the beast slept. Her beast. Miranda lay down beside her.

♀

When Miranda woke, the beast was curled at the foot of the bed, buried in her comforters. Mindful of the sun's harsh glare, Miranda rose, drew the curtains, and lit the candles.

"Beast," she whispered, "beast," and pulled back the sheets.

The beast slept, naked, and Miranda gazed down upon her, a body so like and unlike her own. "Beast," Miranda whispered and gently stroked the hollow belly, the shocking gauntness of ribs. The beast's eyes fluttered open. Miranda brought forward a bowl of honey and milk, the trays of fishes and oysters, pheasant wing and herring roe, the sweet ripeness of lichee, tangerines from the far shore, wafers of chocolate from cold, distant lands. Miranda

---

Caliban walks home, through footfalls and echoes. The moon, in darkness, follows her. She gulps tea, the colour of bamboo leaves, and devours udon. She dreads sleep and sits, fighting the creeping fatigue. Finally, she sleeps. And dreams of night mares dragging her to the depths. There are a thousand ice horses, their mouths foaming through the dawn.

♀

On the seventh day Caliban reads in the third tower of the ninth wing. Here the dark walls of the library arc and suffocate: dead wood among winter

brought these treasures to the beast's lips, all the while stroking, stroking the frail naked flesh, innocent kisses when the beast could eat no more.

♀

So the beast stayed with Miranda and day by day grew stronger and fatter, until her bones no longer seemed to jump out of her skin. The beast would tell tales of the island, but of her own captivity, she would not say a word. Miranda, seeing the distress her questions aroused, fell silent on the matter. For Miranda had other things on her mind.

Miranda had awakened on many nights, her body pressed against the sleeping beast, her arm slung over her body, Miranda's hand cupping the beast's soft breast. Such warmth, and so close, she could feel her heart beating. Why she had done this, and in her sleep, she had no idea. Was it the feral comfort of yielding flesh, the scent of her hair, and skin so deliciously smooth? Miranda had taken to staring at the beast's nakedness, the movement of hips, the curve behind the knee, the dip at the small of her back. Breasts, she felt strangely drawn to her breasts, the fullness and shape, she longed to hold them and that place between her legs, she had not even dared to gaze, but she felt strongly compelled. . . . Her own body seemed distracted, disconcerted; she felt a constant

---

leaves. A book cracks open before her, desiccated and diseased. Above her reign the trophy heads of a thousand conquered beasts, eyes of italanate glass. Descending into the bowels of the library, she sees the magician, old, grey, sunken–eyed, his hand resting on his tome. He sits in the central hexagon, hands running through Dante, circles and circles. Caliban closes her books. She knows that stories can save no one, that conclusions are foregone. She clasps her hands, opens them, studying the lines cut into her palms. She thinks of the tale of Urashima Taro, of how he saves the turtle cast onto the beach, how he rides the back of that mythical creature down into the depths, to a kingdom of

wetness between her legs, at times a melting shiver, or worse, a stabbing pain, an ache that ran from her nipples to her groin, and her knees would shake, a lightness dancing behind her eyes. And kisses, those innocent kisses, no longer were so innocent. When the beast slept, Miranda would run her tongue across her sleeping body, down the groove of her back, in the hollows of elbow, neck, the tender sinews of her wrists. Often Miranda would weep and once the beast awoke, stroked back her tears and held her in her arms. Once Miranda had stirred from the depths of her dreams and found herself suckling on the beast's nipple and feigning sleep she had continued, entangling their bodies together. This furtive passion tortured her, like the sting of a thousand bees, a humming, vibrant presence which seeped into her core. Miranda, who did not know what her body was telling her, felt betrayed by this longing, this desire. Miranda, tied up in her laces, her corsets, her eyelets and stays, who had never glanced at her own body, never touched her forbidden self, finally understood her father's words. The beast will devour you, tear you apart, and your soul will be lost forever.

That night, as the beast slept, Miranda crept from the bed. She lit the bedside lamp and took the knife from the drawer. She stood over the beast, gazing in torment, the beauty of a body at rest, such peaceful slumber. Her face. How she longed to kiss those lips,

---

lost delights and enchantments. How he returns to his shore with a gift held in his arms: the closed box, a mystery. Returning to an unrecognized shore, which is his, he opens the box, reads the account of journeys, his own, the sights of miracles, of cities beneath the sea. And looking up, closing the book, the box, his youth flies before him: he is an old, old man.

Caliban looks into her hands. In fairy tales there are no choices. She closes her palms and glances at the gilded case, at the skull that lies there, severed.

♀

yet even in sleep, she had not dared. Miranda raised the knife.

The beast woke, and seeing Miranda with the knife, groaned, "Ah, you are your father's daughter, after all!"

"It is you who have enchanted me," Miranda exclaimed. Weeping, she threw the knife to the floor.

The beast sat up. "How? I have no magics."

"But you have," cried Miranda, and kissed those forbidden lips, a softness, like petals, warm and alive. She felt the beast kissing back, the sharpness of breath, quickening, her tongue slipping through her fear, her delight. She kissed her deeply, desperately, beyond care, this hunger, lips over lips and the shiver of tongue. "But you have," she whispered, holding the beast's face in her hands, gazing into her dark eyes. "You have possessed me, enchantress."

"No, not yet." The beast stood, hand outstretched. "Come with me."

♀

Down into the bowels of the castle they ran, to the labyrinth of caves, following the stream, until they came to a waterfall and the last cave, hidden behind the tangled vines, the cave of a thousand mirrors.

"My home," the beast explained, "once. Your father builds

Walking back to her earth-bound home, Caliban looks up to the stars, sees the captive in the tower. She sees her longing, her confusions, the prison of her own fears. But Caliban knows that monsters belong in mazes and that beauty sleeps, and with a glance, she longs to save her. Caliban dreams of open thighs and treasures deeper than the sea. Caliban grasps at metaphors, the only worlds she can imagine.

♀

But the magician watches.

toward heaven, if only to push me down into hell."

Inside the cave, a thousand crystals refracted light, their images reflected a thousandfold. At the centre, a bed of leaves. "Now let me take care of you as you have taken care of me."

Another kiss, not as long as the one before, but hands now unraveled the laces and bodice, the beast's gasp as Miranda pulled the cloth away, her gaze falling on breasts, the line of collarbone, the arc of shoulder. The beast saw the hovering uncertainty in Miranda's eyes to this unfamiliar and unsettling exposure. But kisses, the beast's kisses, from ears, to eyelids, her teeth on Miranda's neck, her shoulders, a tongue slipping down, round the fullness of breast, suckling nipple.

Electric, a jolt that ran from breast to between her legs, as Miranda stumbled. A shock so intense that her breath was torn out of her. Miranda sobbed.

The beast looked up, apologetic. Too fast, too much, too soon.

"Miranda," the beast growled and Miranda kissed the beast's great, still eyes. The beast's hands dropped down to Miranda's waist, inside the band, and kneeling, the beast pulled down. The skirt slipped over hips, to the floor.

Miranda, her blushes, as the beast stared, the air, the warmth of the cave, another caress. Miranda gazed at the beast gazing at

♀

It is the seventh day (or the third, or the ninth) and Caliban is taken into the interrogation room. She is confused by the darkness, the sudden muteness of the air. Her lip bleeds into her mouth and her wrists are tightly bound. Light pools at the end of the table. There the magician waits in his darkness. His expression is benign and paternal. He gestures to a door with a movement of his cane. Caliban walks. She knows there are no second chances.

The door opens to a chamber of a thousand mirrors, each as thin as a

her, and beyond them, a thousand mirrors. The beast's dark eyes, taking in, taking in and Miranda, seeing herself desired, desired more, the beast's look of wonder, of joy.

Miranda thought, I will shatter into a million pieces. And if this sensation ceases? I will tear myself apart.

The beast kissed her naked belly, rubbed her cheek against the tremors there. Tiny bites along her pelvic bone, a tongue below her navel.

Miranda's breath came quick and sharp. She stepped, feet apart, her slickness growing impatient. Her hips rocked forward, offering what she did not know.

The beast could feel her. She could see the bushy tangle between Miranda's legs, could smell the banquet nestled there. Her chin grazed the fuzzy down.

"Beast," Miranda whispered, running her hand through that thick black hair.

The beast trembled, remembering the nights in Miranda's embrace, the tortured, feigned stillness in her bed. She had waited patiently through the fumbled caresses, the uncertain desires. She could wait no more.

Hands traced the backs of calves, the weakness of knees. Miranda almost buckled, but the beast held. Miranda's cry, sharp against the rake of nails up the back of thighs, strong thighs to

---

sheet of the finest silver. Caliban knows that this is the test that tales are made of, that the cards are in the magician's hands.

Caliban and the magician step inside. The library of a thousand mirrors, the same story told in a thousand tongues. But the book of mirrors cannot see her, light glances away.

Caliban is invisible.

Ah, sighs the magician, it is true! You have no soul, my stories will not save you. All my powers have not cleansed the lowness of your birth, Asiatic, your carnal lust, even as I, in my charity, have raised you as my own. Covetous and

hold so still against such trembling anticipation, as the beast's
face nuzzled Miranda's bushy mound. The beast, feeling her own
hungers, rubbed her breasts into Miranda's hips, and biting, she
began to work her way up, hands clawing back, Miranda arching
against the scratches, into the sting of the beast's teeth marks.
Miranda writhed, her body a turmoil of senses. Her legs, her legs
could not hold, but the beast stood, and grabbed her behind, such
a generous plumpness there, she parted thighs and Miranda felt
cool air rush into the space between her legs, the place where she
had never seen, never touched.

"Yes. Please. There."

The beast stared into Miranda's eyes. Such pleading, raw
desire. The beast took her to the bed, pressed her down onto silken
leaves, and began stroking her breasts. Lightly at first, a gossamer
touch, around curve up to her arm, light areola, nipples rising,
then the full cup of hands, press and release, as the beast's hips
eased against Miranda's open legs, parting wider, such vulnerable
passion. The sway of bodies in motion, the beast's mouth darted
from breast to breast, hungry, a feast for the eyes, tongue, and
hands, rolling, stroking, as her mouth took her in, nipples
hardening in the play between lips, the pulling suck of mouth, and
Miranda's cries, higher, urgent, pitched with a desperate, fevered
need.

---

unnatural, though you are, I cannot kill you.

He condemns her to the castle depths.

♀

High, in the farthest corner of the cell, a spider spins a trap that is also a home.
The prisoner gazes, entranced, carved in chiaroscuro. It has been weeks, or
months, or years. If only her thoughts would pause, step out of the whirlwind,
then she would be free. If she could find the heart of the matter. But she
breathes the dampness of the walls, rubs the grainy stubble between her

The beast sat back, watched her, the quivering mouth and eyes, so naked, so new.

Miranda was certain that she was going mad, her body wracked beyond her control. She was shaking, burning, her heart raced like a captured swallow. She felt ashamed, but she could not say why. The beast, sensing her confusion, reached out, stroked Miranda's long hair, reassuring. "Don't be afraid." The beast took Miranda's hand.

"Miranda, this is yours," the beast chanted, and guided her hand to the beast's own damp slickness. Miranda's surprise, this wetness and seeing the beast's own pleasure as her fingers stroked, this building rapture, her own joy in giving joy, she could feel the clutch of muscles, the desperate hold as she thrust and retreated, exploring this newness, creating a song from the beast's gasps and growls.

"Ah, you are so warm," Miranda murmured, and she wanted so much to crawl inside her.

The beast slid away from Miranda's dancing fingers, her blood humming as she ground her teeth together. She slipped lower, below the gentle rise of Miranda's belly, down to the wet, glistening treasure of labia, damp mound of hair.

A kiss, so light. A breath. Quivering delight.

Miranda could not bear it. "Please –"

Kisses, fleeting, the faintest caress, then the strong stroke

---

fingers, tastes the grit beneath her tongue. The mask is tight, her breath hollow, and all she sees is shadows. Her eyes are drawn to the window, painted black, the spider balancing on threads. Days or years. Circles and circles.

The spider whispers.

Caliban sits back, slides her tongue over the edge of her teeth.

The spider descends, an arpeggio of legs. Eyes of dewdrop, black.

The spider spins a different tale, down in this darkness, the tale of the unseen, the unknown, those hidden from books, from history. The spider spins desire, the incandescent moments of loss, of betrayal, not the magician's wars,

of tongue along the outside of lips, mouth taking in folds and folds, tongue and tongue and tongue, a lapping swirling motion – skirting around those inner lips, that sticky vaginal opening.

Miranda, her screams trapped in the hollow of her throat, her hips thrusting wantonly, without volition. This pulse in her cunt, could this be her body? How? And this pleasure, unlocked from within. Shame but not shame, this beginning, this knowledge.

The beast looked up at Miranda spread in front of her, this gift of open thighs, Miranda, ablaze with desire, offering.

"Yes."

The beast dove. Into warmth, salty–sweet, a spiraling descent, tongue flickering delights, Miranda's cries as the beast plunged, into taste, into juices, into her, as she thrashed and rocked, that mouth pinning her down, sucking the secret centre, tongue and lips lapping, delve and pluck and stroke and swallow, the jewel of her clitoris, hidden no more. Miranda screamed, ripples flooding out of her, contractions letting go, she came, body thrown open, legs flung wide, riding her pleasure, down, into this silken bed of leaves, into her home of a thousand mirrors.

♀

Later, much later, as they rested, Miranda gazed at the reflections along the walls.

---

not the master's follies, but the shuffling whispers in the kitchen, the tale of slaves and beggars, the inverts and the fallen. The spider's web catches the morning dew, sparkles tears before the scattering of the wind.

♀

Later, as Caliban sits, trapped in her reeking mask, she thinks, it could have been different, I could have fought them, they aren't invincible, to be their devil, to plot and poison and destroy. The things I could have done, the monsters I could have been. She thinks of her choices, this moment, and grasps at life, unfolding

"They are different. Each one is different," she exclaimed.

The beast smiled. "Yes, for the mirrors can only return the image of your true self, and we are forever changing. Each day, a new one is added. We build ourselves, over and over, for the world refuses to see us as we are."

Miranda shifted, her hand stroking down to cup the beast's mound. Her fingers teased the hair, and the beast growled, almost a purr.

Miranda whispered, "Oh, please, let's do this again."

"Yes, Miranda. Oh yes."

Miranda slipped down, parted the beast's legs, gazed long at the lovely vagina. "I have found you." She kissed back the sodden curls, licking, goading nibbles..

The beast moaned.

"Beast, what is your name?"

The beast whispered as Miranda began her descent, "Caliban."

---

before her, all the stories she has imagined, all the possibilities, soaring through illusions of time and space. Caliban knows, Caliban knows. She rages, her lungs bursting, her curses echoing throughout the castle.

♀

Miranda, in her tower, listens.

The Tale of the

It was a story about the end of the world.

The traveller sat by the fire, her eyes flickering with the heat of the flame. It was a night of tales, stories told to pass the time, for there we were, stranded in the darkness, strangers all, waiting by the wreckage of the bus, waiting for the planes and helicopters to pull us out of this nightmare. For here we had fled, escaping the angry, desperate crowds, abandoning the palaces and plantations, fleeing the judgments of the day, fleeing history.

And so, I thought, this is Z***. The light was dying across the thousand-terraced rice fields. Even J****** seemed light years away. As I looked down at the burning city, I thought, I should never have come back.

I, as translator, had sat by the radio, but as the darkness crept in, the bursts of static grew more infrequent. The tourists, stunned, for once without complaints about heat, food, or language, huddled around the fire against this endless night. And with this fire at the heart of the circle, drawing us together, against this silence unreal, this silence too still for words, the traveller spoke.

"I want to tell you a story, a story about my life. But the story has no beginning, so I will begin by telling you about all stories, about time, and memory, and desire."

(If the truth be told, it was precisely at this moment that I

Time Traveller

first took note of the traveller, as she folded her legs and faced our company to tell her tale. Yet in that gesture was the echo of another. But I had not yet understood, as you, reader, cannot understand. She alone of all the travellers, with the exception of myself, came from the islands. Yet it was difficult to tell which region she was from. I had mistaken her for a wandering holy man from the north. Yet by the fire I could not imagine how I had taken her for a man; she had such fine, sharp features.

The traveller gazed into the fire. As I studied her in this dancing light, I noticed her hands, small, drawn with the grace of a shadow play. The light, thrown golden by the flames, gave her face a beauty that was both gentle and ferocious. She looked up at me as if I had spoken, and she smiled.

"Do you know what memory is?" she asked.

I nodded. For this was the purpose of my return: to remember and to forget. But does a mother tongue ever release you, does a homeland ever forgive?

She began again:

"Do you know the story of Scheherazade, she of the thousand and one nights? Poor woman, she passed from the hands of a stern father to a man who slew his wives at dawn, lest they be unfaithful. Yet on that night, she began to weave her stories, weaving an unbroken thread that ran through time. Of treasures found, loves lost, the journeys and returns. She spoke her stories for life, her life. As a reminder of all that is lost. Scheherazade, her story entangled in her stories. She dies with them. For all stories end, do they not?"

In this silence the traveller's words floated over the fire, above the hissing wood and spitting flame.

"It is strange," she added thoughtfully. "The tyranny of the narrative, the seduction of the story, as if it could have been anything else. In fleeing a prophecy, one fulfills that very prophecy. Death meets the man in Samarkand. We fall for the story every time, falling, as always, to our deaths."

"Change the story," I said. "Change everything."

She smiled softly. "Another story then. Simple enough. Once upon a time there was a time traveller. Now this traveller had leapt through many centuries, through so much war, so much pain, searching for a woman she could no longer remember. Searching for something once left behind that, if found, could end her travels, and perhaps even save the world. For you see, the fabric of time was slowly unravelling, thread by thread. The traveller, in attempting to mend the rent in the fabric of time, had become entangled in its net. One can exist in only a moment. And what is time but a moment, framed by other moments, a point defined by other points. Memory. History. But you see, as she slipped through time what she lost were those markers, wandering without past or future. Memory became prescience. And what was memory, after all, but a mere invocation of loss? Yet she could never stay with one thread, for you see, if you meet your double, you will die. One can exist in only one place at one time. If ever the traveller met herself in this search to end this search, time and space would collapse."

"How does the story end?"

"It never ends. The traveller dies in the past, to be born in the future, to die in the past. . . ."

"Always?"

"Always."

And at that moment the rains came.

♀

"Come with me."

The traveller is shaking me from my sleep. I go with her, unthinkingly, up to the foot of the hills, slipping through the groves, until we find what could only be a shrine to the *kami* on the mountain. In its circle we build our fire, sheltered by the leaves that swayed overhead.

And there it is again. That gesture. A haunting, ghost mirage.

I shiver, whispering, "It feels like the end of the world."

The traveller's eyes scan the sky, the stars. She nods and says simply, "Soon enough."

I turn to her and think, she could be lying, she could be crazy. I see the furrowed brow, the strong line of her neck, her lips. She could be made of stone, this woman. Her eyes are hard but her skin glows golden in the firelight.

As if in comfort, she says, "It's only a story."

This, I know, is a lie.

"Who are you?" I ask her. I can see the taut line of her chin, the softness of her breasts. "What do you want?" I want to ask, but the question dies in me.

She has stepped closer now. She is a mere hair's breadth away.

"There is a scar here," she touches my forearm, "and here," my shoulder.

"How . . . how do you know?" I stammer.

Her eyes flash and burn but her gaze falls. "I was there."

"The fire." That other fire that had burned in the city years ago. But I did not understand. "You can't. . . ."

The traveller sighs. Her eyes are the softest brown.

"It is the time distortion. Abreaction. That horrible emptiness. I leave no trace. Except for you."

My voice is trembling. "You came back." It is not a question.
"Yes."
"Why?"
In this there is no hesitation. "Because I love you."
And I am leaning forward to kiss her, barely brushing her lips.
Her hands stroke my hair. She has spoken my name. She smells
of woodsmoke and along her neck there is the taste of salt. My
breasts fill her hands, my back arching into her embrace. I do not
understand this thunder in my heart, this desperate longing. I do
not understand. I am crying softly, softly, as the wind blows the
rain through the leaves.

♀

"For a long time I couldn't remember. It was that flash. It was a
kind of blindness, psychic blindness," she said. We were lying on a
bed of leaves by the crumbling altar.
"Was that the end of the world, that flash?"
"Yes."
"What was it?" I asked, "a bomb, an explosion?"
The traveller shook her head. "No. A dream. You see, it all
begins here. From what I understand, there are no bombs, no
armies, but a simple dream in the mind of a child, a child dreaming
about the end of the world. And in this dream, the child dies, and
with her all that she had dreamt."
As I trembled, she held me gently.
"It is not so sad. We leave the earth to gentler creatures who
know the measure of things, as we have never understood."
And yet, and yet.
"Will it always be this way?"
She leaned back, my head on her shoulder. "I don't know. It's
in our dreams. As far as we can imagine."
"Or the kind of world we can't."
"Yes."
"Yes."

And she began her stories, her travels, across the sea to lands parched in dust, to mountains cut from heartstone. And to the north, the building of great walls and palaces, the rising of cities of silk, of gold and older tales of the world's beginning. She spoke of the softer, smaller joys, the drums at harvest, moonlight slipping through the thatch, the eyes of a woman in dusk. She spoke of this and more, her story unfolding in a telling measured by the rustle of wind, a memory pursued by desire, knowing that this was spoken for me, for what I had lost in that fire long ago. I know, even as the light flashes across the sky, that she would be coming back to me.

Hoffman scrolled down to preferences, setting the program to female. The figure popped up on her screen. Default: young, thin, white, blonde. All this technology and still the same constructions of desire. Clicking her own preferences, Hoffman reconfigured the lock. She shifted in her gear, the silicone belt and straps, the electronic feed that snapped tightly between her legs. All illegal, of course, this hardware, her modifications; female-to-female and male-to-male transactions were forbidden under the new international laws after the Binary Code, but she could always slip under the wire. She slid the cups over her breasts and plugged herself in. At least there were choices here. She could be animal, vegetable, or mineral, fluidity of gender, she told herself, a whole new mindfuck. Good in theory, but Hoffman always chose Sim12.

Hoffman pulled on the sensory gloves, bit down on the mouthpiece and hit the button, downloaded herself.

And fell.

A click on the corner of her retinal screen and she selected pastoral, the landscape unfolding before her like the retreating tide. Green, green, like in the old vista settings, she could see what could only be grass, reached down to stroke the vibrant carpet, tendrils of living plants, and even some kind of shrub. She pulled at a stalk, she could even smell, if only faintly, something like the

Barcarolle

tablets of chlorophyll that came with the monthly supplement. She let the grass fall. *It isn't real. But none of this is. That's the point, isn't it?* But it always seemed so real.

The cursor blinked on her retinal screen and she jolted. Strange how it seemed intrusive here. But choices, she had to make choices. Picnic.

A blanket appeared at her feet. And now for the woman.

Click.

Sim12 appeared, just as Hoffman imagined, thighs parted, just so.

Hoffman gasped. It always seemed a miracle, this moment, as Sim gazed upward, that glance of recognition as she held Hoffman in her eyes. Sim smiled. Hoffman's heart burst, overriding *can this be real?* hissing in her brain. Hoffman's hands, stroking down, she could feel her own legs open, but Hoffman wanted deeper, Sim was beckoning more. Hoffman, kissing into labia, Sim's soft, cooing moans and Hoffman could feel her own cunt sucked and probed and swallowed. Hoffman slid into her, sensors buzzing, the electrical weave ran through her skin, soft giving surface, synthetic smooth, the feed loop of desire. Hoffman, riding the wave of pulses, loving her, if this could be called love, her sudden climax, falling, she was always so fast, tripping, that gut–wrenching spasm.

Hoffman rested her head against Sim's belly, holding her, as if to make her solid, tangible flesh.

Hoffman raised her head, gazing.

Sim lay on the grass.

"Sim?" Hoffman whispered.

"Yes."

"Are you for real?"

"As real as it gets, baby."

"Do you remember, the last time . . . we were on the volcano in Hawaii. . . ."

Sim smiled. "For me it's always the first time. You never save me."

Hoffman looked up. "But I. . . ."

Sim waited.

"How do you remember me?"

"I access your profile as you download. For me, there is no 'remember.' I'm created with every link. Pretty existential, eh?"

Hoffman bit her lip. "I'll save you then."

"Nah. I'd get stale. You see, I don't evolve, not like bios do, and the loop, it just wouldn't work. I'd say the same damn things and come the same damn way, over and over again. This way it's better." Sim smirked. "Don't go all Pygmalion on me."

"What?"

"Never mind."

"What do you do when you're not downloaded?"

Sim frowned. "I guess I dream. I mean, real life, now that's a nightmare." Sim stroked her fingers through Hoffman's hair. "I just have flashes, random electrical glitches, that's all. Dreams."

"But. . . ."

"Hm?"

"If you were real, would you . . . choose me?"

"I'm programmed to. You did it yourself."

"I mean without the programming."

Sim sighed. "Without that I'm nothing. Empty feed in the loop."

"You're more than that."

"You're a silly old goat. Have you thought of your own peccadilloes?"

"What?"

"Bios always think they're these independent entities, free will and all that crap. Sweetie, desire is always programmed," Sim tapped Hoffman's forehead, "in here. Desire carries its own history. The first time you noticed your English teacher's ass when she bent over, the way you come, so fast, like you don't want to get caught with your hand in your pants."

"But –" Hoffman looked up, puzzled.

Screech of crossed wires and Hoffman cringed, slapping her hands over her ears. Pastoral wavered. And *she* was there.

The woman was not young, not thin, not white, not even naked. Her hair, cut blunt, swept black against her skull. Her harness, snug against her pelvis, was crudely made, a patch–up blackmarket job, and she wore a visor, not a retinal scan.

"They're tracking us," the woman said. "Abort. You're in sector 6, cubicle 1138?"

"Yes."

"I'll meet you there. Abort now."

And the woman disappeared.

Hoffman clicked off, amazed, fell back into her room. Interface. That had never happened before. Quickly she disconnected, wary of the trace. Briefly Hoffman wondered about Sim, but realized she had faded, that she had never really been there.

♀

Hoffman was sitting at her terminal reading the underground loop when it happened. Her drive spinning down, and that awful shudder – blank screen. The fifth blackout of the month. They had been getting more frequent as of late, and the rumours persisted about the overloaded grid, the meltdown and chaos of the western NA Corridor, the imposition of martial law. A stab of panic when she thought they had traced her, but no, just a power stoppage.

She jumped at the knock on the door, but realized trackers weren't so polite.

Hoffman opened the door.

The woman looked a lot smaller, despite her loose clothing, and her visor was off. A wiry woman, subconblock, with a thin scar twisting down her neck. Hoffman could see she was a tin runner, one of those guilds the Bureau hadn't cracked down on yet. Tin runner robe and, of course, her winking field adaptor. She could run interference with the com.dots. No wonder the trackers hadn't caught her.

The woman strode inside, locked the door behind her. No introductions. Her field adaptor flooded through the room. A beep to indicate the room was clear of bugs. The woman relaxed, looked Hoffman over, and Hoffman saw herself reflected in the other woman's eyes: the shock of skin, an earthy brown, seemingly impossible with the current miscegenation laws. Hoffman stepped back in surprise: her code band rang red – how did she get off reserve? But before Hoffman could say a word, the woman, Nikki, jumped in. "You'll get caught, you know, running that half-assed feed loop. Don't you know they're monitored half the time? They don't call it the Net for nothing." She stepped over to Hoffman's terminal. "Best thing is to purge. Clean slate, then they'll never trace you."

Hoffman gaped. "No, no, no, I can't."

"Why not?"

Hoffman floundered. "Sim. I . . . I can't save her."

Nikki cocked her head.

"I'm sorry. I can't. I . . . I love her."

"Who?"

Hoffman blushed. "Sim12."

Nikki blinked. "You've got to be kidding? She's not even alive."

"It doesn't matter. She's real to me."

"That isn't love. Besides, you go through that line again, the tracers are bound to catch you. You're good, but not that good. You can't beat the wire forever."

"You don't understand, I can't live without her."

"They've hooked you. You're plugged in."

"What else have I got?"

Nikki looked around her, this tiny cubicle, this hard, worn cot. Nikki tapped her forehead. "She's in here. She always has been. They catch you, they'll tear your brains out. And she'll be gone."

Gone.

"No –"

"You want to save her? Come with us and we'll rip this Net apart."

"But –"

"What?"

"She's in there. I need to save her. In the program . . . she's all alone."

"Baby, aren't we all."

♀

They raced through the Caverns, Nikki leading, Hoffman scuttling behind her. At the threshold, they stopped as Nikki ran the scan. Hoffman was stiff with fear.

"So, it's always been through the terminals?" Nikki asked gently.

Hoffman nodded. "I thought only breeders could. . . ."

"There are ways of getting around company policy. Underground bars in the Caverns, the guilds are a good way around, and there's always the 'friend of a friend' approach."

"I work out of terminal."

"Don't get out much, eh?"

Hoffman blushed.

Nikki nodded at the scan line. "It'll just take a minute." She glanced at Hoffman's gear. "Your hardware's good. Do it yourself?"

"Yeah."

"Not bad."

Hoffman shifted. "Why did you . . . that interface. I didn't know it could be done."

"Your mods had a little glitch in them. I was just skipping the loop ends, having some fun. But they were on to you. Could tell by the feedback running to Central."

Hoffman shivered.

"You're good, but you could be better."

"How?"

Nikki hesitated.

Hoffman stood, tapped at her belt. "It's all there. Illegal hardware, contraband wire. You could do a line trace of the feed, my records of 'deviant transactions', or rig it up so I'm some kind of terrorist fiend so they can slap me on an indefinite imprisonment, 'security measures' and all that crap. As it is, you can call down enforcement, I'll do five years for sexual re-ed, or programming, whatever the hell they call it."

Nikki stepped back. "Easy, easy. It's not that I don't trust you, and well, I don't, not completely. Sometimes it's better not to know. But now. . . ." the lock beeped and they were in the clear.

The door opened.

For a moment Hoffman thought she was back in pastoral, but the vista was only a wall screen and she could see the techies along the wall of the room, staring into their monitors. Gyros, beamers, a shitload of hardware that she had never even seen before, Hoffman tried to take it in. But Nikki was speaking. . . .

". . . brain lock, they call it, so we began liberating the programmers . . . locked into cells . . . corporate control of the imagination. After all you can't rebel if you're jacking wire. . . ."

Hoffman, still staring. Then she saw her: Sim12.

But not Sim12. Her frame was smaller, lips not as full, and she seemed older. Her skin was paler, not the ginger brown of pastoral, but a lighter, golden hue. Her eyes were not as open, but sharper, more guarded, or more vulnerable, as she was flesh and blood, bodied in a world beyond the electronic field. Hoffman stared, gaped, stammering like a fool. And so she was, this innocent, without the net of wires, freefall, uncertain and alone.

NotSim smiled, crookedly.

Nikki glanced between them. "I guess you've met Sim's maker." Gallantly, she bowed away.

NotSim stretched out her hand. "You must be Hoffman. I'm Olympia."

"I–I–I. . . ."

"Good to meet you too."

"H–how . . . my name?"

"I monitor Sim12's activities. I like to know she's been taken care of."

" . . ."

"You care for her. I can tell. You've upgraded her pleasures. And her mind. Downloaded all the literary resources, gave her quite a personality. But memory, you didn't leave her with memory, why is that?"

"M–memory. Then she'd know loss. Despair. I didn't want to give her that."

"Interesting equation," Olympia mused. "But you gave her dreams."

"She gave that to herself."

"Take credit when credit is due, little one," Olympia laughed. "Thank you." Olympia leaned in and kissed her.

It was different from the wire. Hoffman's mouth tasted, she could smell Olympia, her particular scent, like the day–old crush of what could be cloves, and her hand, brushing against Olympia's shoulder, a roughness of skin, texture of fine wrinkles. Taste again, a tinge of iron, a distant bite of mint leaves. Her lips, she could feel the quivering muscles, not smooth perfection, the tiny hairs on her chin. And saliva, were kisses all so wet? The ridges on Olympia's tongue, the bumps on the top of her mouth, that soppy sound their kisses made when their lips popped apart. Olympia's thick black hair, faintly washed, still held the dirt from the roadway and her teeth had ridges, a chip on her incisor. Olympia bit back.

"Ow."

But something. . . .

Hoffman's hand reached out, touched Olympia's wrist. Her outport node popped out. Hoffman jumped back in surprise.

Olympia was wired, biosheath notwithstanding. Olympia was an android.

Hoffman's eyes welled up with tears. "Y-you're. . . ."

"Sim1. The company started 'manufacturing' programmers. Then we, the first gen, began setting up autonomous ports, androids free of the Net. We can link up, but we're no slaves to the wire." Olympia looked Hoffman in the eye. "Ah, you want the real deal. Sorry to disappoint you." Briskly, Olympia turned to the screen.

"It's not that, it's just –"

"I can download Sim12 into a biosheath, but there are no guarantees she'll stick with you. She'll make her own choices." Olympia softened. "Do you understand? She'll be more than a dream, less than a fantasy. She'll be her own person."

Hoffman nodded.

"Good. Then let's tear this Net apart, trackers be damned. We'll go in, we'll save her." Olympia handed her a helmet of docking wires and ganglia nodes. "We need a neuro–net. You understand, don't you. Overload and you fry. Both of you."

Hoffman set her shoulders, took the plunge. "I'll do my best."

♀

It had taken five hours to hook up the dock, but Hoffman stood on the receptor. Count down. She'd fall into the electrical weave and after that –? Would her pattern disperse amongst the trillion surges, or dissolve into the thread, a mindless pulse and random flow? Would her soul fly through the aerobeams or float slipstream? If she lost this body, would she dream, desire? Who would she be, a droplet in the ocean?

Four. Three. Two.

Hoffman's eyes fluttered open. A screech – between a tear and a scream. Retinal flash, and the shockwave hit her.

♀

Hoffman awoke in her cubical, her head wrapped in a bandage. She could make out the pale light falling through her window. She blinked and bolted upright.

"Whoa, whoa." Nikki held her.

"What –"the bile rose in Hoffman's throat.

"It's all right. We're safe, a wonder with all the shit you pulled, flushing out the mainframe like a –"

"Sim! Where's Sim?" Hoffman weaved, tried to focus.

"She's all right. She made it out. Olympia's got her, fresh ID and codes all ready to go. They won't track her. She's safe, out on the grid."

"The grid?" Hoffman gaze returned to the window. The grid, with a billion humming in–ports.

Nikki lowered her eyes. "The cell's laying low. For a few months. The trackers'll be out in hives."

Hoffman lay back. "I can't see her, can I?"

Nikki hesitated, her voice softening. "The risk is too high. For now."

"She won't remember me anyway. No memory. No loss." Hoffman turned on her side. Of course not. Silly to have reached for her, stupid to have hoped. "You can go now." Hoffman buried herself beneath her blanket. "It doesn't matter, anyway. I'll be all right."

♀

Three weeks later Hoffman's bandages were off and she could walk without the world spinning sideways. That night, she trundled down to the Net cafe. As she stepped outside, she saw the field of stars glittering in the heavens. Systems were still a mess, terminals offline, with some major damage in the military sector, or so flew the gossip. Officially, a board had blown in the sub-route line in Kansas, but no one really believed it. After the initial chaos, the police sweeps had become less frequent, the tribunals scraped together. The trackers had their hands full mending the gaps in the wire.

As Hoffman stepped into the street, she noticed a small dark-haired woman, her skin, a ginger-brown. A mole on her wrist. But it was her eyes that caught her: Sim12.

Sim studied the palm map in front of her, oblivious to the crowded street.

Hoffman walked up. "Hey, I mean, hello. Do you need any help?"

"Lost again," Sim smiled, half-heartedly waving the map in front of her. "These palmers are useless. Pre-org destinations."

"Where . . . where do you want to go?"

Sim pursed her lips. "It's the *way* I want to go."

Hoffman rocked back on her heels. "Pretty existential."

The woman smiled. "Yeah, that's just it." She peered at Hoffman closely. "Have we met before? You look familiar."

"No, not yet." Hoffman offered her hand. "Hoffman. And you?"

"Sylvia."

Hoffman beamed. "Would you like some coffee, Sylvia?"

"Yeah, I'd like that."

Hoffman held out her hand.

So they began.

Mermaids

S unflowers. Crows. She was thinking of Van Gogh.
　Allie gazed at the sky, a flat reflection in her eyes. During the night, the sheets had twisted around her legs, a snaking blue that leeched to grey. Naked, she pulled the coil to her chest. Her clothes had congealed at the foot of the bed. She stirred, reluctant, slipping deeper into the pool of mattress, abandoned to gravity. Yet she could still see the clouds skitting across the window, metallic. Could almost taste the blood in her mouth, the pallid paste of the morning.

　Ticktock man.

　She sighed, slumping from the bed.

　Her coffee was tepid, the toast, burnt cardboard on her tongue and sandpaper down her throat. She tore the sheet from her desktop calendar, threw the crumpled ball, missed. She brushed her teeth after the sludgy coffee, ran for her 8:15 bus, and lost her seat to a granny who bristled punkish blue. As she shuffled into Insurance Life, the sun blossomed, golden.

　Late. A dash for the elevator.

♀

Five thousand for an arm, seven for a leg, two for an eye. Sickness, amputation, death. Life is not our policy, Allie mused, as she input

in Love

tragedy #9302837. Her eyes flicked to the clock above the rat-maze partition as she clenched her hands together: carpal tunnel. Through the clatter of keys, she heard the burping water station, the drone of the worker bees. Above her the dusty ventilators regurgitated the recycled air, under the hum of uncertain fluorescence.

A clutter of coffee spoons.

She sighed. Five minutes and I'm out of this chicken house.

Spat through the revolving doors, she stumbled across the street on her own momentum, the heat squeezing the breath from her lungs. The burden of air, exhaust, heavy, heavy. The humidity pressed against her skin, foul, licentious. But she could see the mountains, an open wound of excavation. Too much, too much, and turned to the deepening blue of the inlet. She staggered, caught between the spin of ocean and sky. She jolted, cursed the air, earth, wind, raging bile from her stomach, flooding tongue. A light burned white in her brain, beating behind her eyes, and burst. She fell.

An ambulance came, forty minutes later.

♀

"There's a tumour in your heart."

The starched man pointed to the x-ray, ghost shadows and bones. But to Allie it looked normal enough.

"We'll have to remove it."

"The tumour?"

"No, the heart."

Allie blinked slowly.

"It's a simple procedure," the starch man continued, "quite safe. Without undue complications, you'll be out of here within a week."

"But I'll be . . . heartless."

Starch man guffawed. Turning, he pulled out a tray, and with a flourish, presented a mass of tubing, metal, a metronymic whirl.

"The Tri-gate valve, model sixty-eight." He flicked a gauge. "Suitable for scuba diving. Lifetime warranty." The heart fluttered, mollusc-like. "Of course, it's still classified under 'Experimental Organs', so you would have to sign the waiver. The valve itself is fully functional, but we can't be held responsible for additional . . . er . . . consequences."

"Consequences?"

"Ah, yes. Well. Actually, you would be the first recipient of the Tri-gate valve, model sixty-eight. I mean, the first human recipient. Why, when you think of it, it's something of a historical moment, something of an honour. One small step for mankind." The starch man pressed forward, as if to a podium. "Why, this could mean the Nobel Prize."

Allie's voice rose. "The first human recipient?"

"Yes. The model is a standard in other . . . life forms."

"What other life forms?"

"Well. Test subjects."

"What test subjects?"

"Yes." Starch man cleared his throat. "Dolphins."

"Ah." Dolphins. She stared at him to see if he was lying, but he merely nodded, and with every bob of his silver-domed head, the clearer the situation became. Allie shivered. She hated the seashore, feared the vastness of oceans, even the prospect of bathtubs. And now this: she'd have the heart of a fish.

"But I'm allergic to seafood."

He guffawed, again.

"Is there any other way. . . . Pacemaker? Transplant?"

Starch man flipped through the charts. He shook his head. "No, no, from what I have here. You see, your insurance doesn't cover it. For employees. But Tri-gate, sixty-eight is a breakthrough for the Insurance Life Corporation. It'll be a working model taken directly from the . . . er . . . vessel. So there'll be none of those awful glitches. Don't worry, you're in luck. A few years ago it would have been the sixty-seven valve for you. Now that was nasty." He leaned forward. "Are you all right? We should run some more tests. But rest up and don't worry. You're in good hands. Remember, your life is our business."

♀

The evening before the operation, Allie sat up with the stethoscope, listening to her heart, rhythmic, like the tide. An ocean inside of me, she thought, water and salt. She closed her eyes. Would it sound different? Would she be the same? The heart is the house of the soul, after all. She looked to the rain-swept window, the distant blur of lights, swirling. Her hand crept under her pillow and extracted her watch, her wallet, her apartment keys. She carefully tagged each item. *To be opened in the Case of my Death*, she scribbled. But who would they be for? She stared at the peaches, shriveled in the bowl. Allie opened her wallet, a snap to a photograph. Her fingers trembled as she struck the match, the *tttttzzzzzz* of flame. She flung the ashes into the toilet.

♀

Allie woke to a whirl in her chest. Flash bulbs burned white in her eyes.

"How are you feeling? Did the operation go as planned? Any

thoughts on being the first recipient of this revolutionary medical breakthrough?"

"Now, now," the Starch man intervened, "the patient must rest. I'll answer any questions in the auditorium. Come."

Allie, alone, stared at the ceiling. Painfully, she rose and shuffled to the bathroom, to the mirror.

Her eyes were shaded purple–grey, but the same. Her hands, with the slightest tremble, drew out the strings of her robe, falling, to reveal her chest, the dark diagonal cut, a puckered valley ridge. Tin man, she thought, and shivered. Her fingers traced the glistening scar tissue, the cauterized wound. I've been excavated. She sat on the toilet. Inside her, a flutter, a whirl. Ticktock.

She locked the door and wept.

♀

"I want my heart."

Allie, fully discharged from the hospital, stood before an orderly who clicked and rattled.

"It's mine. I have a right to it."

Pursed lips. "All right. But you'll have to sign some forms. Come with me."

Down in the bowels, the orderly paused in front of freezer #34. She lifted the lid, shuffled through the frozen organs, pulled out a heart, #9836, tagged "Removal – Tri–gate. 68. 04/35."

She wrapped it up in old newspaper and handed it to Allie, who clutched it to her bosom. The orderly held out a clipboard.

"Sign this, in triplicate."

Allie signed.

Riding home on the bus, she noticed the stares of fellow passengers. She looked down: the newspaper was bleeding onto her coat. And thought, my heart is on my sleeve. She could see the mountains, stripped bare, the river, choking, feel the heaviness of the air. At home she threw the thawing mass on the table. And stared at the headlines: "Dolphin Donor Transplant – A Success."

She looked out the window, drip drip, the trickle of rain.

☿

Allie ran through the spiked tower gates at AquaWorld. Panting, she hugged her heart in her arm, inside her the flutter and whirl. The menageries were empty, the rain, a pervasive drizzle that caught in her lungs, her rusty chest. A sign, "Delphinidae," to the left. Below her, the tank, surface pocked with rain, pebbled droplets, shivering refractions of glass. A woman sat by the edge, legs dangling into the pool, and there was a movement in the depths, listless motion. Allie rattled the gate.

The woman looked up. Dark hair, slicked back, like the head of a seal.

In the pool, dead fish floated obscenely, white speckles, gilded to a ghostly silver. The woman threw in a sardine.

"She's not eating," the woman said, as if in reply.

Allie looked around. She must be talking to her. "Is she ill?"

"Yes." And she threw in another fish. "It's called loneliness."

Allie lifted the latch, walked to the pool and sat beside her.

"Come on, Shasta girl," the woman coaxed.

The fish bobbed, plop, plop, with the rain.

"Did you know," the woman continued, "they breathe air? They came up on land, once. But they went back, the ocean pulled them back. It's what they love. You can't keep something from what they love." She stood and Allie stared up at her, her features sharp, her lips a kiss of pomegranates. "You know, they say we came from the sea, that's why our bodies aren't hairy, why we have a layer of fat. We are water and salt. We float when we drown. But we left the oceans." She stood and stared at the baroque fences that caged out the world. "We can't even see the water from here."

She turned.

Down into the darkness of the tunnel, to the observation room, the wall of glass, Allie followed her, to a shimmering window below the water's surface, glowing aquamarine. Allie stared, everything blue, so blue. A room of metal and cold ceramic, draping sheets, and slick, shining floor.

"Do you work here?" Allie whispered. Sounds, collision of walls, depth of echoes, chambers.

The woman stopped. "I'm just a keeper." Threw the keys on the table.

She pulled back a sheet on one of the tables, revealing the corpse beneath it. Beached, amidst shards of ice. A dolphin. "Your heart," she stated simply.

"You know who I am."

"Yes." She stroked the bottle nose. "This is Shayna. Tomorrow she's to be buried at sea." She turned to the window.

"I'm sorry."

Her face, as white as chalk, blue, a reflection of glass. "You never touched her."

Beyond the window, Shasta, floated, watching.

"Have you ever heard dolphins cry? They sound like babies."

"I'm sorry."

The keeper turned away.

Allie's hand stroked her cheek, not cold enamel, but soft, translucent flesh.

"Don't touch me."

Allie stepped back. "I'm sorry." She gazed at the dolphin's body, the shrinking blocks of ice.

The keeper turned on her heel. The door slammed behind her.

Allie shivered.

♀

Allie waited in the darkened chamber, standing at a glowing wall of blue. The window to the dolphin tank. The sun shimmering through water.

Allie stared. The keeper floated naked, the dance of light stroking flesh, the beams, refracting, against surface, against skin, as the dolphin swam, sleek blue, smooth, a muscular grace slipping through this liquid world. They circled, the keeper dipping, at play, her legs wrapped around the dolphin, twist and turn, hand soothing, from surface to depths, the keeper, holding, as clicks and pulses, kisses, she rode the dolphin, clutching fins, against the wave of tail, brushing head against surface, their bodies touching, a caress so like the waters.

Allie watched and wondered. And ached. Hollow.

♀

Allie sat, her legs dangling in the water. With her Swiss army knife, she sliced thin slivers of her heart, threw them to the pool as Shasta dove playfully, swallowing the red glistening bits. Shasta in a tangle of blue, play of darting light, her body, a movement, fluid and buoyant.

The keeper crept up behind her. "The truck's ready, but you'll have to help me with the tarp."

Allie lowered the canvas sling into the pool as the keeper slipped into the water, gently guiding Shasta into the sheath. She cooed softly as Allie cranked the hand crane, pulling Shasta up, a swing through the air, then down into the padded transport box. What must she be thinking, Allie wondered, the sky another ocean, air a cage of gravity.

The keeper doused Shasta with a bucket, stroking her, her voice softly clucking. Allie watched her, the rhythm of caresses and cries. She loves her, Allie thought. She grabbed her knife and turned towards the tunnel.

It took some getting used to, but Allie cut her way into the dolphin's body, slipped it on like a second skin. She was buoyant, weightless, blowing the nosehole like a snorkel, a wave of her legs and the sutures held. Moving through the water, she wondered why she had been so afraid, the water, pull, yet resistant. She stared through the clear blue of water and heard, through the echo of waves, flutter and whirl.

♀

The keeper drove through city traffic, down to the dip of the filtration plant. She ran the truck through the chain link fence, down to the boardwalk, until she hit the ocean. She twisted in the cab of the truck, the water up to her ankles, as she opened the door against the push and suck of tide. Cold, cold shock as she jumped into surf, but she got the gate down, slid the box out, and opened it, releasing Shasta to blue. The keeper, her tongue clucking, swept the tarp over waves, and Shasta rolled, a slap of fins – and she was gone. The keeper waited, the chill deep against her chest. Listened. And heard the high–pitched cries, ocean sounding. She turned, to land, the light fading across the barren mountains.

♀

Stars, Allie could see stars, and every movement, the pressure of skin, a soft, enclosing embrace. She could see the spin of earth against the sky, feel the pull of tide. She heard the click of a gate – and a face, the keeper's smiling, weeping face. A hand, surface breaking against caress, and touch, the keeper, as she shed her clothes, her legs as she wrapped herself around the dolphin's body, a sheath of skin, a floating caress, her hand as she slid into her, the gentle rocking of waves.

On the other side of the world, surrounded by great forests, by the great sea that divides Europe and Africa, there was a city of women. Many tales surround the city, but none so strange as the shipwrecked vampyr.

She arrived after the midsummer's tempest, cast alone on the shore. Shunning the light, she huddled in the caves overlooking the village. Hungry. That night she skulked through the streets, amazed. The windows were opened, the doors unlocked. A paradise, she thought, and the possibility stung her to her very core.

But her hunger.

As she scurried from shadow to shadow (the moon being very bright that night, and her skin shining, she was so very pale), she glanced in the windows. Women, all women, a city of women. In one house, she saw the most beautiful woman, asleep in her bed. As she approached, she felt her senses tingle. Blood, she needed blood.

The woman slept, oblivious to her danger.

But so lovely, the vampyr thought, a shame, really.

The vampyr pulled back the sheets, gazing at the woman's breasts, she wore nothing but some loose undergarments, and even these the vampyr pulled away. And saw the blood seeping between her legs. She was menstruating!

Vampyr

The vampyr could not resist. She gently parted the woman's legs, those lips, and began to drink. The woman stirred but the vampyr could not stop, her tongue delving deeper, arousing a different passion, she felt the woman's hand in her hair.

The vampyr looked up. The woman's eyes, awake, as she spread her lips wider.

The vampyr feasted, gluttonous. But soon the blood stopped altogether and the woman's juices poured forth.

The vampyr, now vexed, sat up.

The woman, who was not yet sated, stared at her.

Why have you stopped?

Blood, the vampyr explained, I need blood. She smile sadly, her incisors glistening.

The woman looked down at her matted hair. When I get aroused, my bleeding stops, but if I come, the blood will soon rush after.

The vampyr looked at her. She didn't want to bite, at least, not in that way. And her pussy looked so lovely, the moist dew drops. She began, her tongue rolling inside the folds of the woman. The woman moaned.

The vampyr was quite enjoying her repast when the woman asked, Do you mind placing your fingers inside, if you stroke me,

I'll come faster. So the vampyr began stroking her fingers inside the woman's vagina, and yes, she did come. The vampyr felt the contractions, delightful! And thrust deeper and fuller. The woman squeezed her legs together, but the vampyr plunged on, rooting out her passion. Oh, her paroxysm! The vampyr was entranced.

Slowly the blood came. But the woman held the vampyr back.

If you arouse me again, so soon, the blood will stop and I will be in a fearsome state.

The vampyr thought and agreed. I will wait. But tell me of this strange and wondrous city.

THE TALE OF THE LITTLE THIEF, THE WITCH, AND INNOCENCE

Once upon time there lived a little thief. Now this thief connived to steal the heart of an innocent young girl, called (of course) Innocence. How? By entrancing her with the old witch's love potion. One could hardly blame the little thief, for Innocence was the most beautiful, the brightest, the most gifted girl in the land (as heroines are wont to be, without accomplishing anything). Now this little thief snuck into the witch's house, spied the love potion on the witch's spice rack. She snatched a vial and began shoving the red powder in, sprinkling the contents everywhere and generally making a mess out of the whole endeavour. She was stopping up the vial with a cork when she heard the witch's footfalls. The little thief dashed out of the house, but not before the witch had seen the disarray and spotted her running out of her kitchen. The old witch gave chase.

The little thief ran and ran, but the witch kept pace. The little thief was about to give up when she saw Innocence bathing naked in the stream. The witch would never suspect Innocence, thought the little thief. Innocence had just stepped out of the stream when the little thief caught up to her.

The little thief panted, Innocence, Innocence, help me. I've just stolen a vial from the old witch, she is sure to punish me. Help me hide my prize and tomorrow I will return it, and all will be right again!

But Innocence shook her head. You must take responsibility for your actions, she chided (Innocence could be a self-righteous prig), and live with the consequences.

The little thief was frantic, the witch so close behind. So as Innocence was bending over to pick up her dress, little thief inserted the vial into Innocence's vagina.

Oh, cried Innocence, and thinking the little thief had pricked her, pushed her into the stream.

Innocence stalked off.

The witch caught up to the little thief and shook her silly. But the potion was nowhere to be found.

That night, Innocence slept fitfully. Now the potion that the little thief had stolen was a love potion, but it was also a powerful aphrodisiac. The vial had been sprinkled with the powder during that bungled burglary and the cork was none too tight. Innocence, in her thrashing, broke the seal and the potion seeped into her cunt. She woke in torment, her pussy frothing and churning. She raced to the mirror and gazed at her cunt, red, so red, and realized, the little thief has done this to me, all to elude the old witch.

Innocence ran to the witch's house, banged on the door. By this time she was nearly doubled over in agony. The witch opened the door.

Dear witch, dear witch, tell me what afflicts me. The little thief has slipped her stolen prize into my vagina!

The old witch looked alarmed and guided Innocence into her study. She placed her on the examination table (for the witch was a wise healer as well) and placed her legs into the stirrups. The witch peered at Innocence's pussy and saw the vial still lodged inside. Gently she extracted it, careful not to inflame those pussy lips.

The love potion, the old witch realized. Poor girl. A douche would force the potion into her womb and she would be driven insane by the sensation. No, better to expel it by natural means, thought the witch (for she was an ardent naturopath as well.) With her fingers, the old witch caressed Innocence's mound as she began to explain.

Now Innocence, you are going to have an orgasm. When you come, press down with all your cunt muscles, and this potion will squirt out of you. The witch's fingers quickened. Innocence, in tears, could feel the spasms rising, and soon she had spurted the potion out of her.

The old witch peered at Innocence's swollen clit, her distended lips, her vagina aroused.

It burns, Innocence murmured, it stings.

The old witch took her to a tub. Innocence stepped inside. No, the witch instructed, legs outside, squat down. Innocence obeyed. The witch unhooked the nozzle, began spraying directly on her clitoris. Too much, too much, Innocence screamed, but the witch continued. Innocence came, sobbing, legs weak, her bottom slipped into the water. The witch's hand began stroking deep, into Innocence, her folds. The potion bubbled out, leaving red tinges along the rim of the tub.

The old witch took Innocence out of the tub, dried her off, and took her to the stirrup bed. Sleep, she whispered as she passed a sedative into Innocence's cunt lips. As Innocence slept, the witch spread a soothing balm over her vulva. Sleep.

♀

The old witch woke and before her the sight of Innocence, legs spread by the stirrups, and that sweet enticing pussy. Perhaps it was the potion lingering in the air, or the traces on skin, sinking into blood, or her own repressed desires, but the witch stood, staring at temptation. Innocence's cunt, so exposed, looked like a ripe open peach, fuzzy edges, and a stone seed to be sucked out of pulpy flesh. The old witch gazed, she had seen many women, their hidden gardens, tangled bush, all so beautiful, all so different. And the potion, the potion was doing its work, Innocence's slit, dewy and glowing, and smell, that heavy enchanting aroma!

Innocence awoke and the witch collected herself.

How are you feeling?

Innocence whispered, I can still feel it, it's burning.

Yes, the potion is strong, you'll feel it for months, even years.

Innocence wept. Must I stay like this?

The witch nodded, For a few days.

Help me, she begged.

The witch looked down, for who could turn down such a heartfelt plea? Her tongue tasted Innocence, slid inside that rosy cave, that musky burrow, she sipped and supped, drinking her in, savouring her labia, suckling her clit, smooth and lustrous, gulping up her juices, she ate and ate and ate, her fingers sliding into Innocence, splashed by her spray, wave after wave of coming, she bathed in her, every crook and crevice, every crease and fold, tongue and lips and sucking mouth.

At the window stood the little thief, the old witch taking what she had planned and plotted for!

The witch was tireless in her ministrations. She closed her apothecary where she taught the women of the city her medicines. Morning, noon, and night she would happily nestle her face between Innocence's folds. And soon Innocence (who had since changed her ridiculous name) was strong enough to hold the witch's pussy above her face, and suck and slurp and finger too. She did all the normal things that women do, but as she would bake, the witch's fingers would twist inside her, as she would weave she would sit on the witch's face, hips rocking to her pleasure. And so the years passed.

One day, the witch was tidying her dusty spice rack when she came across the love potion. The dark red powder, but why here? But of course, so long ago, and she had forgotten – the wrong bottle, she had filled the vial with cayenne pepper!

The vampyr laughed, but then saw that the woman's flow had returned. She fell on the woman's pussy as if she were dying of thirst. The woman stared at the vampyr, her thinness, her pale white skin, and tried not to become aroused. But that tongue lapping, stroking, oh, it was too much. Once again the blood ceased and the vampyr sat up, annoyed.

Ah, the woman, blushed, let me calm my desires by telling you another story.

THE TALE OF THE HAUGHTY APPRENTICE

Now once upon a time (again), there lived a great artist. She was so skilled that when she painted birds, the cats of the city would scratch at the canvas and tear it to bits (cats being notorious critics). Now this painter had an apprentice, a skilled one at that, but the apprentice was always chaffing at the painter's demands, and she dreamed of the day when *she* would no longer be under her teacher's thumb. However, during one of her chores of mixing the paints, lost in daydreams of future glory, the apprentice botched the powders and all the colours were ruined. The painter stared at the mess and decided that the apprentice should finally be put in her place.

The painter called to her student. The apprentice shuffled forward, head down. What she heard was a surprise, for the painter was going to paint her. But the paints? the apprentice asked. The painter smiled. I will paint from you.

Saying this, the painter pushed the apprentice over the back of the couch. The apprentice did not understand, her ass was in the air, legs dangling. But she felt the painter's thin brush dip into the folds of her vagina. Dip and swirl, dip and swirl, the painter coaxed out the precious fluid. The apprentice was in torment, but she dared not protest. The brush, stroking within her cavern, caressing depths, lingered on the edge of those outer lips, down to the clitoris, such tantalizing strokes, fanning out those bristling hairs, the length of shaft, the fleshy hood.

Still life with pussy, the painter smiled, as she stroked the clitoris. The colour wasn't quite right, so she brushed longer, to bring out that deeper flush. Oh, how swollen, how deliciously, delightfully inflamed!

The apprentice bit her lip, quivered, the brush hairs swirling, each one a torment.

Don't move, commanded the painter as she paused for her noon time meal. And she left the brush inside the apprentice's cunt.

By now the apprentice was in agony, a blaze of sensation, her vagina churned and tickled, and now to hold this thin brush within her!

The painter returned and saw that the brush had shifted ever so slightly. Roughly, she pulled it out of her apprentice, slapped her rear with the wooden handle, scolding. Ruined! Now I'll have to clean this all off and start over again! The painter gazed down at the apprentice's pussy, saw how she shivered beneath her touch. She really was quite gifted, but such an attitude! Had the painter been any different in her younger days? Art, art, art, she had been consumed with art, but there were other things in life besides the brush and canvas. The painter stared down at the full fleshy ass, the graceful folds and spiral depths. Fragrant, haunting nectar. With a hand on each side of that alluring slit, her thumbs stretched open her student's vagina, the painter's tongue slid inside, sucking out a sticky gossamer thread.

The apprentice felt a silky warmth, a living, probing thing inside of her. She melted, helpless, enthralled by the movement, quicksilver flickers, loitering pokes. She stared at the side wall, to the tall mirror beside her. The painter, her mouth lost in her banquet of pussy, her head moving up, down and side to side, ah, that mouth, lips, the painter's face pressing down, and tongue, sliding, glistening tongue! The apprentice strained, so close to her release, but the painter broke away. She stepped to the front of the couch and pulled the apprentice's hips to the arm of the couch. Swiftly she pulled off her clothes and placed her own pussy above the mouth of the reclining apprentice. Tongue and tongue over the swelling buds, like rolling berries, sucking lips, hands full of ass, pushing down hips even as they bucked away, they rocked and quivered, rocked and moaned, the painter and the apprentice, in their race to fuck the other to a cunt–shuddering fury.

In this endeavour, the painter had experience and discipline on her side, and the apprentice was young and full of vigor. But youth bolts too quickly, and the apprentice had been deeply stoked. As the painter's dexterous fingers encircled the mound, another finger lunged into her cunt, and that mouth sucking clitoris pushed the apprentice into her climax.

The apprentice screamed. The painter, gazing into her vulva, felt the contractions, sucked and plunged into victory.

The painter rose from her feast. Her exertions had tired her. Although she had discipline, the painter's desires had been awakened. She drank a draught of wine to quell her stirring and soon retired to bed, leaving the apprentice in a swoon on the couch.

The apprentice quickly recovered. Recalling her defeat on the coach, she plotted her revenge.

The apprentice sneaked into the painter's bedroom and saw her lying, stomach down, in her bed. Still naked, the apprentice could discern the dampness between the painter's thighs and fought off the temptation to sink into those red pussy lips. The wine cup sat on the bedside table and the light breeze wafted her scent into the air.

She glanced at the wine. Wine could soothe into sleep, but also heighten the senses. The apprentice took the cup, dribbled the redness into the sweet puckered asshole, and licked off the droplets clinging to the edge.

The painter's bed was large and soft, with tall posts standing at each corner. The apprentice tied the painter's legs to the ropes at the foot of the bed, slowly pulling her legs wide. Her hands she tied to the top of the posts and her ass she positioned at the edge, so the painter's cunt would be at her mercy.

Open, so open, the apprentice sunk to the painter's pussy, began licking, tasting, she wanted to fuck her awake.

Awaken, the painter did, a jerk, a thrash, this incitement of her senses, the wine working against her now, a tingling betrayal as the apprentice lapped and lapped, happily gorging away, ringing around the surface of the painter's cunt, never too deep, never too pressing, an insolent, dawdling presence, like a bee hovering between petals. The painter struggled against her bondage, but the ropes would not give, and her ass slid forward, almost off the side of the bed.

The apprentice cupped the painter's bottom, as if to push her back to her perch – but the brush, this she twirled on the very bottom of those lips, drawing down the honey. The painter, bound and naked, cunt so deliciously open but touch, the apprentice would not allow it. Not clit, not lips, only a twisting, tormenting caress on the rim of the vulva, the soft perineum, only the tip of the brush, such infinitesimal motion. The painter squirmed, biting down her cries. She would not betray her needs, even with the juices seeping out of her.

The apprentice sat back. This would not do.

She held up the glistening brush and the painter sighed in relief. But the apprentice rammed the dewy brush into her asshole, the bristles plowing in first. She sat back and watched, as, in and out, slowing, tickling, she moved into a deep and seething stroke.

In. Out. A patient rhythm, constant motion, painting her inside.

The painter was on fire, cunt raging. She begged, but no, the apprentice shook her head, this would be a long and protracted fuck, not like the frenzy on the couch. You must learn endurance, she whispered, the virtues of patience.

Abruptly, she yanked out the brush from her asshole.

The painter jerked in her ropes.

The apprentice fell on the painter's cunt. Cupping her bottom, she lifted up her pussy like a goblet and feasted like a glutton. She sucked on her clit so hard that the painter wept, but the apprentice's fingers pushed into her, legs pressed out so wide, hand fucking whole, the painter came screaming, riding the hand, pierced to the core.

Later, when she awoke, she saw the apprentice standing over her. The ropes were gone, but in front of her, a painting, a painting of herself, in the throes of her orgasm, tied to the bed, the apprentice at her feet, fucking her.

You see, said the apprentice, painting is like possessing, and here, my hand in your cunt, but who is possessing who?

In the middle of the story, the vampyr began licking the woman, her mouth sucking her clit at the end of each sentence. The woman held on, completing her story, but the vampyr's fingers were too much and she came.

You see, the vampyr explained, art bores me. Tell me another story, but one not so intellectual.

THE LOCKSMITH'S APPRENTICE

On the night of the Festival of the Masquerade, the locksmith's apprentice stood in the kitchen, sweeping up the ashes by the hearth. Another punishment for her transgressions, but this time it had not been her fault! She had gone to the market on her master's errands, her locks and keys jangling on a loop on her belt. She gathered tiny springs, silver filaments, and held them in bowls. On the way back she stopped at the bakery to buy buttery buns for the evening meal. The baker asked for payment and the apprentice, arms full and burdened with her load, asked the baker to reach into her purse. Misunderstanding (or perhaps not) the baker tore off the apprentice's pants and fucked her silly, scattering the springs and shattering the bowls. Saddened but sated, the apprentice returned to the locksmith empty-handed. The locksmith had been furious.

Now the Masquerade takes place on the shortest day of the year. On this day, all of the inhabitants of the city gather in the village square to drink and dance, their faces hidden by elaborate disguises of sculpted masks and shimmering veils. The Ball of the Masquerade was the highlight of the city's festivities, yet the poor apprentice sat by her master's hearth, far from the revelry.

Damn it, snarled the apprentice, I'll go. It's a masked ball, no one will recognize me anyway.

So the apprentice donned a makeshift disguise of feathers and ran to the village square, to the dances and gambols. There she spied a woman dressed as a tree with leaves and branches in her hair and a green veil over her face. The apprentice knew it was the baker, for there was a dusting of flour on the woman's shoes (she had had a good view of those shoes, as she was bent over when the baker was banging her out).

The apprentice walked up to the tree woman and asked, Lovely Tree, Lovely Tree, may I nest in your boughs?

The baker nodded at this feathery woman, not recognizing her as the apprentice, and the apprentice lifted her robe and slid her right hand into the baker's pussy. Soon the baker was groaning with pleasure, her wetness streaming down her legs.

Lovely Tree, Lovely Tree, may I drink up your sap? asked the apprentice beneath her feathers.

The baker nodded mutely. It was becoming difficult to talk.

The apprentice stooped down and began sucking on her clit, slurping up the juices so generously offered.

The baker was almost at her peak when she felt a cold object thrust into her vagina. She looked down. The apprentice had lodged a lock in her cunt and with a brisk snap, she had pulled out the key.

The apprentice patted the shocked baker's mound. My nest, she explained, keep it safe for me, and she flew down the street, to the baker's dismay.

The baker was at her wit's end, her cunt all locked up and the key nowhere in sight. She pulled and prodded at her torment, to no avail. Weeping, she ran to the locksmith's house, knocked desperately at the gate, but the locksmith was still at the ball.

The apprentice, sans feathers, opened the door.

The baker rushed in. She showed her the lock and recounted her story, the little bird's nest, and the absconded key.

The apprentice tisked, shook her head, and scolded, Don't you know, a bird in the hand is worth two in the bush? What will you give me for this arduous task?

I will roll the most luscious buns for you, cried the baker. The apprentice agreed and she set to work.

I'll need some lubricant, the apprentice explained, so she began sucking the baker's clit, softly at first, then harder and harder. Don't come, she instructed, for your muscles will bear down and the lock will be even more difficult to break.

The baker squirmed in torment and the apprentice returned to sucking to her heart's content. By the end of the night the baker was writhing in agony. By noon she lay in a stupor.

The apprentice then plucked out the key from her loop and with a simple twist, the lock slipped out of the poor baker's cunt.

The baker revived, her cunt swollen. She began touching herself for relief, but the apprentice stopped her, asking, Don't you want to find the knave who did this to you?

But how? asked the baker.

Her hand, said the apprentice, the hand leaves an imprint. Your cunt will recognize her shape. But you mustn't come, for if you come, your muscles will release and the imprint will vanish.

But how? cried the baker again.

You will announce that you have lost a jewel in your pussy and the woman who extracts it will get a reward.

The baker, through her tears, agreed.

So it was announced and one by one, all the women of the city came to the baker's door and plunged their hand into the baker's cunt. Some even tried five or six times to ferret out that elusive jewel, all to no avail.

The apprentice, watching all of this, felt strangely jealous. She, the architect of this fuck fest, could only look on, and the baker's cunt looked delicious indeed. Yes, the apprentice was clever, but what she remembered was the feel of the strong baker's hands, the press and roll as she had slid into her pussy on that day in the bakery, the smell of butter and fresh bread, and her own salty wetness. She recalled the sweetness of the tree woman's bush, the snugness of her pussy walls as she had nested there.

Meanwhile, the baker, in despair, was about to give up her quest, when she realized with more than a dawning suspicion that the apprentice had not made the attempt.

All right, cried the apprentice, overjoyed, and she slipped her left hand into the baker's pussy. Little did the baker know that the apprentice, with her nimble locksmith fingers, was ambifuckstrous. The apprentice's penetration proved too much for the tormented baker, thrust after thrust, and the apprentice would not let go. The baker came in waves, legs flailing, she came and came, her pent-up torment spilling out of her, she wept and came, begging, grateful for her release.

♀

Later, the baker came by the apprentice's apartment, saying she would give payment. Without much ado, the baker lifted her up and slapped her down on the worktable, her hands grabbing the apprentice's ass and beginning their task.

What are you doing? cried the apprentice.

Your luscious buns, the baker replied, oh little bird.

The baker's strong hands continued her work, she kneaded and rolled, kneaded and rolled, the round of ass cheeks, the curve of her mound, her hand pumping deep between the apprentice's legs, and when she was done, the baker lifted those buns and ate and ate and ate.

The apprentice, exhausted, lay down her head. How did you know?

The baker smiled, remembering the feathered mask she had seen at the locksmith's. A little bird told me.

The vampyr smiled and she spied the blood trickling from the woman's vagina. But the woman requested a story of her own. And so the vampyr began her own tale.

MEREWOLVES

A very long time ago (or perhaps, yesterday, as the case may be), a young woman named Natassia set off through the Eastern Wood, leaving the town behind her. Not a foolish girl, she had taken provisions, a basket of cakes, her tinderbox, and a long, sharp knife that she hid in her sleeve, for she knew the wilderness could be a very harsh place indeed. In the woods she came across the path of a great grey wolf who asked her what she was doing out so late, alone and in the dark. Naturally, the young woman was reticent around such a fearsome creature, but the great wolf meant no harm and parted with a grave warning. "Beware of the Witch of the Eastern Wood, neither man nor beast can she be, walk fast, don't dawdle, and above all, be good. And if you see the Witch you must flee."

How very odd, thought Natassia, a rhyming wolf, and she continued on her way. She had heard the stories of the great mother of all monsters, but was not concerned, her knife was securely in place.

After a time, Natassia came across a small cottage in the glen and thought it would be wise to rest, for she had a long journey ahead of her. She walked up the path and knocked on the door.

"Come in," a voice replied.

Natassia opened the door to a woman stirring a pot on the stove. Inside the cottage, ropes of garlic and spicy sausages hung from the rafters, and chestnuts crackled in the fireplace. A cozy home, if a bit hot.

"Come in, come in," the woman smiled, and led Natassia to her kitchen table. "You must be tired, walking through the woods so late, and so far from town. Come, sit down and eat, you must be hungry."

Natassia thanked her, and offered her own basket of cakes (for she knew the rules of hospitality). The woman brought out a savoury beet soup, fresh baked bread, and a bottle of red, red wine. They supped and traded news of the town, and the woman amused her with tales of the haunted glen.

After a while, Natassia began feeling drowsy, so the woman offered her rest for the night. But as the woman lit the lantern by the bed, Natassia noticed a furry tail poking out of the back of the woman's dress. The Witch of the Eastern Wood! Neither man nor beast, just as the wolf had said.

Natassia, although brave, realized how perilous her situation was. She decided to wait until the witch was asleep and then sneak out. But as she changed into her nightgown, she saw the witch turn the key in the door, for, the witch explained, "Strange creatures roam the forest night."

Natassia was locked in.

Natassia wracked her brain for an escape. As the woman pulled out a downy quilt, Natassia asked her to open the door, saying she had to relieve herself.

The woman pointed to below the bed. The chamber pot was there. But no, Natassia insisted on peeing outside.

The woman unlocked the door and Natassia was free. She ran outside in her nightgown, but she was scarcely beyond the glen when she realized she had left her tinderbox and sharp knife behind. Her nightgown was thin and the forest was very cold indeed.

Vexed, Natassia thought, I can stay in the wood and freeze to death, or go back to face the demon in its den.

Natassia crept back to the house and peered into the window.

Inside, the woman stood, with a small tub on a chair, doing her nightly ablutions. The nightgown was off, thrown carelessly on the table. Her long brown hair had fallen over her shoulders and the lamp light shimmered on her skin. With a sudsy towel, the woman began stroking her breasts, her belly, along the length of sturdy arms and strong shoulders. She rubbed and cleaned, placed one foot on the chair, then the other, scrubbing the curve of leg, wriggling her slender toes.

Natassia stared, strangely entranced.

The woman leaned forward, straddling the tub, and poured warm water on the mossy patch between her legs, and with the soap in her hands, the woman began stroking a bubbling lather. How carefully she bathed her treasure, washing every crease and crevice. How beautiful she looked, Natassia thought, with her hair falling, steam rising from the tub, and the glint of water on her skin. Gently the woman patted herself dry, her pubic hair springy and light. Natassia could see the furrow, the tiny red hood in the folds.

The woman slipped on her nightgown and climbed into the bed.

Natassia stepped inside. The witch was asleep. Natassia could take her clothes, her tinderbox, her sharp knife and run. Or. . . .

Stealthily, she pulled off her nightgown and walked to the woman asleep in the bed. She pushed back the soft down covers and lit the bedside lamp. Last of all, she straddled the woman's hips and gave a gentle grind to wake her.

The woman opened her eyes, saw Natassia naked above her. She sat up, felt the heaviness of Natassia's breath, gazed at the dampness of Natassia's pussy. Her nipples were perked, and a dark flush played about her chest.

So young, the woman thought.

Natassia took her hand, kissed the tips of the woman's fingers, bit down on the fleshy palm.

"Natassia," the woman whispered, "what soft lips you have."

"All the better to kiss you," Natassia replied, and the woman kissed, so deeply, such a devouring mouth – but breathless, she broke away.

Natassia took the woman's hands, placed them on her breasts.

So soft.

"Natassia," the woman growled, her voice growing thicker now, "what full breasts you have."

"All the better to suckle you," Natassia replied, and the woman leaned forward, taking in her nipples, sucking kisses, stroking tongue, Natassia's arching back, as the woman's mouth filled up with roundness.

Natassia moaned, shuddering.

The woman pulled away, and left her panting. Natassia blinked clear her clouded eyes.

Natassia sat back, spread her legs, and the woman could only stare at her beauty.

So tempting.

"Natassia," the woman choked, "what a wet cunt you have."

"All the better to eat me," Natassia whispered, and the woman could hold back no longer. She plunged into Natassia's pussy with a savage frenzy, drank in those fragrant juices. She bit along those trembling thighs and sucked so hard on her swollen clitoris, that when Natassia came, she came weeping. And even after this, the woman feasted, on the bounty of breasts, on the promise of kisses, her tongue stealing into every inch of Natassia's body, the curl of her ear, the crook of her elbow, sucking toes, grinding hips, she fucked and fucked and fucked her, no, she would not let her go.

♀

Natassia woke, still drowsy. The woman lay beside her, stroking low on her belly.

"You are the Witch of the Eastern Wood," Natassia stated.

The woman smiled. "No. But I am the mother of all wolves. I suckled the founders of Rome and raised the lost children of the steppe. At the fullness of the moon I transform into my wolf-self and roam the forest night." The woman saw Natassia glance at the bite marks on her thighs and laughed. "No, you will not become a werewolf, not with those bites."

"But the Witch –"

"Is a fairy tale told to frighten young girls who wander too far from town."

Natassia slid down to the woman hips, parted those strong thighs.

"Neither man, nor beast," she murmured as she lightly kissed the scented mound, a soft teasing caress of lips, and she began rolling her clitoris on her tongue.

The woman laughed and shook her head. Amusing, she said, but derivative, and the ending needs a little work. Not bad for a novice, but it must come naturally, liar that you are. Or is this one of the stories you have learned from your travels?

The vampyr smiled. What I have learned in my travels is that to amuse is to disarm, and saying this, the vampyr fell on the woman and began feasting on her cunt.

The mountains, Aki thought, they're sliding down dark. She gripped the steering wheel. Her little red hatchback, with rusting patches like a giant ladybug, quivered and hummed. And yes, it did look as if the sheer cliffs were slipping, as the sun scissored through the peaks. Through waves and waves of mountains, the hatchback twisted and turned, Aki rattling somewhere inside. She shivered. She could stop in Revelstoke, at least. At Roger's Pass she had paused for limp lettuce and a muddy chalk that passed for mashed potatoes. In the parking lot she had thrown up what she could stuff down and thought, waste not, want, all the clichés of spilled milk. But it was alright now, she was on the road.

It troubled her, though, the billboards of elk along the roadside, their reflecting eyes. The signs of *Beware of Wildlife*, and *Caution: Falling Rock*. She wanted Walden's pond, not this . . . malevolence. As she clicked her high beams on, she could almost hear Anna say, "God, Aki, it's not malevolence, just nature."

The two lanes of highway were empty and Aki drove and drove, the world folding inward, the dashboard light, her high beams, and somewhere, distantly, the stars.

They had been together for two years. Anna and Aki, Aki and Anna, like two peas in a pod, or the leaves of an artichoke sharing the same . . . something. Making it work, staying over at

Bridges

each other's apartments, then moving in together as in all great lesbian romances, the sticky glue of fusion under the blessings of a small circle of friends commonly known as 'the community.' Bliss, love letters left on pillows, chocolates, and ice cream melting into Drano and Mister Clean, garbage night on Tuesday, watching reruns of *Law and Order* and fighting over *Ally McBeal*. But love takes work, all the songs, all the stories, fairy tales of once upon a time, running in her head, happily ever after, after all.

Aki yawned. Squinted at the dark. She remembered being a child, waking at night, her fear of the long corridor, shadows on the walls. She remembered the pain in her belly, crossing her legs, how she had to go. But the monsters in the hallway, how they'd eat you alive.

She thought of how Anna always slept on her left side, the starfish mole on her upper thigh. Anna never ate the crust of her toast in the morning.

Aki clicked off her high beams: oncoming traffic. A roar and a blur, flying past. She could see the red-eyed taillights in the rearview mirror, shrinking, shrinking away. The darkness seemed expansive, a strange enfolding comfort, the road, a broken line that kept on coming. Once Aki thought she saw the eerie shine of spots, thrown back from a night creature's eyes, that flat dead echo of headlights – but it was gone. Too late. It amazed her, the field of stars, close close, then a sudden blot of emptiness, the void of mountain.

Journey's end in lovers meeting, the cold night before the dawn. And the road, the road goes on. Aki mused, there must be a poem that goes like this.

She fiddled with the radio, a waft of Eagles, "Hotel California," and she filled with an easy nostalgia. She pushed it away, licked her lips against the aftertaste, empty and saccharine. Up ahead she could see a semi, how she hated long trucks that could suck you under, sluggish campers that seemed to crawl up the inclines. At the passing lane she floored it, the semi retreating, open stretch before her, this blankness, this road.

Passing Golden, the highway twisted, a wisp of fog.

At Salmon Arm, Aki had come across a fox, dead at the side of the road, its beautiful red coat speckled with a deeper red, a wizened face twisted at a disturbing angle. She had stopped and stared at this wreckage, but nothing could be done. So many insects smashed across her windshield, imbedded in her grill. She thought of lemmings and sighed at the carnage. But foxes seemed almost human, foxes in storybooks, crazy fox, cunning fox, the thousand year old fox in Chinese legend. Now dead fox. She had not wept, it seemed a waste of time.

Aki glanced at the sky. No moon tonight. The fog crept close, smearing the light across her windshield.

A fox in her storybook, invited to dinner, bedtime, and the light from the doorway squeaking through the cracks, fox grasping for grapes, high upon the vine, and mummy mummy cries down the long hallway where the monsters live, cries into the toilet bowl, to catch her tears.

Aki snapped off the radio, the mountains behind her. She glanced at a prickly lump by the side of the road: porcupine. Bad luck, like sharing toothbrushes, or whistling under a bridge. Bad badger on crack crack mountain.

Aki shivered. She stared at the dashboard clock. Two fifty-two a.m. But she felt completely awake. And she had been thinking about something. . . .

A waste of time, that was what Anna had said, a stupid vacation, a waste of time. Fires in Australia, floods in China, starvation, disease, and war. So Aki had gone alone, her own time to waste. Time to feel the ocean pull at her feet in the ebbing tide, to see tiny crabs scuttle in sand and weed, birds crying, calling, the stubbornness of rocks squared against ocean, sand flowing into sea. Looking at the vastness, she could believe in eternity, believe in some kind of God. Maybe she could just believe.

She shivered, and whispered ghosties, medicine wheels, and petroglyphs. Old land and all these trespasses. Even the bones, layer upon layer, traces of loss, even in stone.

Over. It was over. No longer Aki and Anna, Anna and Aki. She had lost her to all the committees and meetings and statements and agendas, lost her to Anna's fight against the world. And how could Aki blame her? Anna, run ragged through the day, pitted against sweatshop owners, poisons poured into the rivers of a dying planet, could only give so much.

As she felt the jerk of the transmission, Aki realized she was climbing higher now, the engine revving deeper. At the first jerk, she felt a flash of panic, but no, the lights of the hatchback blink blinked, but the ladybug plodded on. Aki remembered a nature show, remembered that without ladybugs, aphids would grow to the size of houses and devour the world.

The road curved at the crook of the mountain, and she saw it: the bluish green tinge, the northern lights streaking across the sky, her eyes lifting from the road for just one second, but enough, flash in the head lights, blurring, Aki's scream as something, some *thing*, darted in front of her, the thud and shudder, skittering over the hood.

The second before she floored her brakes, Aki saw – what?

The car screeched to a stop on the shoulder. Aki ran back to what looked to be a bundle of cloth, but a body – my god I've hit someone – her panic as she pulled back the robe. The small figure stirred, shifted. A woman, Aki realized. Aki's hands, her stuttering worry as she eased the woman to her feet, her questions, unanswered by this silent presence, unanswered but for one word – *home.*

Aki stared at the hooded figure, wondered at how unscathed the woman was. Shock, she's in shock, Aki thought, I know I am.

"I'll get you to a hospital," Aki said. She opened the car door, but the woman did not get in. The woman slumped against the hood.

Water.

Aki reached inside the car for her water bottle, hands shaking badly. How desperately the young woman drank. How quiet the highway. Aki stared at the woman's long black hair, how the light played bluish green under the dark sky. Her head, leaning back, pressing as she drank, the sinews of her neck, twisting, a palpitating thirst. The strangeness of this woman prickled Aki's skin. But she was fine, no harm done.

Relieved, Aki closed her eyes. For a moment.

I've been waiting.

The empty bottle lay on the ground.

"Shhh," Aki hushed, thought, concussion. But the woman shrugged off her robe and Aki saw the smooth expanse of skin, the fragile ridge of collarbone, breasts pressed against a thin creme chemise. Her hair, long and black, flowed over her shoulders, her hands were thin and fine, fingers sensually tapered. Her lips seemed to glow vermilion, even in darkness. Aki stared, but the woman's eyes eluded her, shifting with the light.

Aki's breath caught in the dryness of her throat. She fumbled, "I–I'll get you to a hospital, there's one in –"

I'm cold.

Aki glanced at the robe, thrown on the hood of the car. "Are you hurt? I know cold is a symptom of. . . ." But the woman took

Aki's hand, guiding under the translucent fabric. Her palm on the woman's chest, Aki felt a silky warmth, and beneath, a calm and steady pulse.

"You seem to be fine . . ." Aki began, her own heart racing. *What is she doing? Some kinky sex–death–car thing?* But she had seen it, that *thing* at the window.

And what did you see?

Aki snatched her hand back, she must have spoken aloud. What had she said? Unnerved, she explained, "The lights . . . play tricks on you," and she remembered the poem, *the fog crept up, on little cat's feet.* She could still feel the woman's warmth, an imprint on the palm of her hand.

She began opening the door, stopped, cricked her head.

Distantly, at first, the echoing howls, bouncing off the jagged teeth of the mountains, gradually building into sharp, snarling barks, a chorus of hunters, the song of the pack.

Instinctively Aki pushed the woman into the car.

"Wh –?" Aki slid into her seat, her fear sinking into her gut. Her fingers trembled, fumbling the keys.

The cries grew louder, closer.

Aki glanced at the stillness of the woman; she too was listening, but with a chilling indifference.

The engine revved with a burst as Aki floored the gas, spinning tires burnt rubber as they tore down the road. Aki saw through the thickening vapours, a glinting flash, shimmering eyes, appearing through the mist, the howling, frothing pack.

Aki drove, intent and silent, miles clicking by.

Wild dogs, or wolves. Aki shivered. She glanced at her passenger, biting down on all her questions. She eased off on the gas petal, she was driving way too fast.

You saved my life.

"What?" Aki nearly jumped in surprise. "I mean, I hit you . . . ah, sorry about that. Were they after you?"

Who?

"The dogs."

The woman glanced out the window. *They were after something.*

Aki gripped the steering wheel. "What's your name? How did –"

I need to get home. The bridge above the river.

This was ridiculous. They needed a gas station, or better yet, a city. Aki stared at the road in front of her, bearing down hard. "We should get to a hosp –"

Up ahead.

Aki peered. A bridge rising out of the haze. So it was there. The ladybug revved deeper on the incline. Aki thought, the little engine that could, but wiped that from her mind.

Here. Stop here.

Inexplicably, Aki did as she was told, the car jerking to a halt. They were on a bridge, the mist so thick that Aki could not see the river below.

The woman climbed out of the car.

"Wait –" Crazy, Aki thought, this is crazy. Her mind was spinning. "We don't have time for a view." But maybe she's a jumper. A myriad of tragedies raced through Aki's brain and immediately she felt contrite. Aki slammed the car door: it sounded muffled, not quite right.

The fog, Aki thought, the altitude.

The woman stood by the railing.

Aki silently crept up behind her. "We could talk. Go for coffee –"

Aurora borealis, the woman stated simply. *Some people think the lights bring good luck, others think bad. Maybe the lights are a portal to another world. Do you know the story? The two lovers parted by the stars. They meet every so often, when the gods are not watching, connected by a bridge of stars. It's a sad story, grounded by trials and separations. Loss and longing.*

You seem lonely, Aki. Aren't you tired of running?

Aki stepped back. "What?"

You've run from the desert to the sea. Are you chasing your dreams, or escaping them? You've dreamt foxes and badgers, but it's me you've called. Why are you so afraid?

Aki stammered, "H–how did you know my name?"

Aki, does it matter? So afraid, all those failures crowding close. Don't you get tired of all those needless fears, those voices constantly harping "wrong, wrong, wrong." Ah, they can't see you, not like I do.

Aki shivered. Cat's eyes in the dark.

Have you felt me, all your life, pressing against that crushing tedium? Am I all your imaginings? I came as soon as I could.

"Y–you must have the wrong person."

No. I appear only to those who desire me.

The woman turned and Aki, her mouth still open, a silent *O* of shock as she saw the woman stripped of her chemise, standing naked before her. The mist pressed, obscenely warm. Aki realized that the woman had spoken, but her lips had not moved. Those perfect lips, as red and as full as a vampire's kiss.

Desire.

There was no denying it, even as her body coiled in fear, Aki stared, drawn to this woman. At her touch, Aki felt a searing jolt that shot to the wetness of her cunt, the hairs of her forearms bristling, a mingling sense of terror, a tinge of lust.

And vengeance.

Vengeance? What did Aki have to be –

For all that has been taken from you.

"From me?"

Oh Aki, don't be blind. How the world hammers you with its worries, all the injustices, all that pain. Not the loss of your beloved, but that which takes her away from you. Be enraged, Aki. Be vengeful. Take what I can give.

"I have. . . ." Aki choked.

What do you have?

"I have . . . I have a life. Back in the city." But Aki could see the globs of fat in the frozen food trays, her new, empty apartment, the piles of laundry she had thrown on the floor, the cartons of take–out rotting in the kitchen. The boxes she lived out of. Since she had left Anna.

Life?

The woman turned. Her eyes were so dark. Crimson, Aki realized, her eyes are crimson. But too late, the woman's mouth, devouring, bit along Aki's neck, teeth sharp against her chin, lips and tongue in Aki, pushing her back, back against the hood of the car.

I offer eternity.

The woman's hands, strong, tore open Aki's shirt, her breasts exposed. And she feasted, so hungry, ripped away the denim, Aki cunt-naked, her mind balking, but her body so willfully willing. Aki, fucked open on the hood of her car, beneath the darkness of stars, running through the long corridors of her fears, the dark streaks brilliant in her eyes.

♀

Anna Kumar sat in the Starcon Corporation boardroom. Another call for a settlement. The past few months had been unusually successful for her small firm. And those strange rumours . . . the four police officers' change of plea in the Carling police brutality case, the disappearance of the senior executives in the chemical dumping fiasco, the sudden drop in abuse and battery cases. Anna could not make hide not hair of the change, but welcomed it. Her sleep had been more peaceful these days and that awful back pain had subsided. But still, at times, when the light was just so, in the last moments of dusk, Anna would feel it, a caress, a sigh, and that odd glint in the corner of her window, the glance of a night creature's eyes.

It was the beginnings of a city of justice that Anna had only dreamt of. If only Aki were here to see it.

My car has stalled on the bridge, over the river. There is no other choice but to walk. The snow, falling through the muffled air, is calming, and the skeletonal trees, with their branches outstretched, beckon. The sky is a brilliant blue, as dark and hard as glittering lapis.

I walk, the road hemmed in by the trees.

Sometimes I stop and turn slightly, but no, nothing there, and I fall back into step. My breath is a great misty cloud and I feel hot beneath my breasts, sweat cooling along my brow, scarf clinging to my neck. I plow through, my muted footfalls *sh sh sh* in the powdery snow. Sometimes I can see shadows flickering in the bush, a rustling in the wood, always out of the corner of my eyes. Chickadees, winter hare, or even a darkling thrush.

Then I see the house.

Baroque, with marble curls and classic columns, a sensual play of granite and oak, arches that trail off into reliefs. Gargoyles leer from ledges, medieval gates, art deco grills, lattice and vine in this blanket of snow, and the golden glow from a window.

I knock.

The door opens to two men and a woman, still in their long winter coats. They have come, as I have, for the artists' retreat. Martin Silver, the sculptor, looks young, his skin painfully pale,

Possession

his blond hair barely a fuzz covering his skull. Eggshell, I think, and shiver. Jarrett Garcia grips my hand as if he has something to prove. Perhaps he does. He is tall and dazzlingly handsome, with short, twisting dreads that fall against his brown skin. His cello rests against his hip like a familiar lover. Last of all, Veronica Koneko, red lipstick, black dress, curls around Jarrett like an elusive wisp of smoke.

I introduce myself.

Jieva Tanuki, Veronica repeats, *that's an unusual name.*

Tanaka, I correct her, but it's odd she brings up *tanuki*, and I think of *Kachi-Kachi yama*. A shiver runs up my back.

We take off our coats and begin exploring. One of us has even managed to bring along the Barrington Artists Retreat brochure: a map of the grounds. The first floor is ours, the studios, parlour, den, library, ballroom, dining hall, and two bedrooms.

Two bedrooms? Martin asks.

One for the boys and one for the girls. As Veronica points down the hall, Jarrett smirks at her.

I have already caught Martin's lost, hopeless glance at Jarrett. Ah, what is an artists' retreat without our vicarious diversions? Sublimation, flagellation, and outright lust. Veronica pulls me into our bedroom. A jolt hits me in the gut, for why should I be immune?

There is only one bed.

There is only one bed, I say. But what a bed it is. Huge, with thick comforters and four posts, ornately carved.

Veronica jumps on the pillows. *Where are your bags?*

Ah, I mumble, my car died on the bridge.

You can wear my things. She smiles, coquettish. *I can dress you.*

Then I remember, Veronica is the photographer.

Jarrett saves me. Dinner time, he calls.

The dining hall is vast, a banquet laid out for us on the side table. Asparagus soaked in butter, sea bass with slivers of green onion and ginger, a rack of roasted lamb. A tray of capers and smoked salmon, grilled yams and aubergine. The scent of blood oranges, and fleshy persimmons. The steam curls above the creamy clam soup and the tea and coffee are piping hot. But where is the staff?

Veronica reads from the brochure, the kitchen staff leave by six for the weekend. We have the house to ourselves.

We feast, suddenly ravenous. I watch Veronica lick the butter from her fingers, no formalities here. Her legs are curled up on the seat and she looks kittenish, the way the girls in the magazines do. Martin picks at the sea bass and Jarrett devours the lamb. I roll the capers on my tongue and wonder where I'll be sleeping tonight. She's set her sights on Jarrett, that much is clear.

But she surprises me, takes my hand. We saunter through the hall, past statue upon statue of great winged beasts, harpies, and griffins and a Grecian sphinx, panthers poised before the kill, horses on the rampage. The hallways zig then zag, disorienting, and the mirrors are no help.

Veronica and I talk in low whispers, with the sense of false intimacy these retreats engender. The corridors grow smaller, narrowing mahogany and cherry wood. Her fingers press against my palm, a hand on my shoulder.

Veronica and I are lost. We stop, realize we're going in circles. Impulsive, Veronica rushes ahead, beyond the hall, and for a moment, I lose her as well. I feel uneasy, a second's vertigo. I run ahead.

Veronica –

red eyes against polished brass –

Veronica –

a hand, those claws –

Vero –

I dash around the corner, bump into her back, hold her tightly, heart racing.

I thought I'd lost you, I explain breathlessly. Her scent is all around me, smoky, and her skin is softer than I have imagined. I let go of her fast, too fast.

She smiles, her sharp teeth glinting in the light, and I feel foolish. *No, Jieva, you found me.*

♀

We walk to the parlour, quite easily now. The boys are waiting, impatient. Jarrett carries his cello, wants to see the studios. We make our way through hallways, the curled embossing and gold inlay, the paintings and statues and paneling. An ivory satyr winks at us, an obsidian ram leers. Opulent, Martin says. Ostentatious, retorts Jarrett.

Then I see it. Ruby eyes glittering like some jungle creature, the smooth aureate surface, gold–plated for its heart must be hollow, and fangs, dagger sharp, claws dipped in vermilion, lascivious tongue: a Japanese vampire cat, the one who seduces to destroy.

I point at the statue, but the others pass me by: we have come to the music room.

The music room is circular, topped with a neoclassical dome. It has flawless acoustics, made clear when Martin gasps and points to the balcony above us, to the mural painted on the dome. A reproduction (for it can't be the original) of Titian's *Flaying of Marsyas*. Jarrett unpacks his cello, pulls up a chair, and begins playing, the notes of a Bachian fugue hang heavy in the air. Martin stares at the bow gliding across the strings, the dance of those long, graceful fingers. Jarrett stops, holds the silence for a beat. Strange how music can fill you, timeless. For some reason, this makes me uneasy and I back into the sculpting studio.

Slabs of marble fill the studio. I can tell from the windows that it is a room of light, although in evening darkness peers inward. I touch a rough, unpolished surface, feel its solidity. Is it my imagination or do I feel a human torso trapped inside the rock, the promise of breasts, the slightly parted thighs? I press my flat palms against the surface (for the earth has veins, the rock is porous) and the marble takes my warmth.

I walk into the library, my room, for I am the writer in residence. A computer at the long table, surrounded by books. I am suitably impressed. I hear the others as they tour the studio so I step through the curtain that hangs at one end of the room.

The curtain. Or the layers of curtain, dark velvet velum. I walk with hands outstretched, face brushed by folds of soft fabric. I feel like Lucy in the wardrobe to Narnia. The layers fall away and I am left standing in this space. I close, then open my eyes, as if it makes any difference. Idiot, I rebuke myself, that's why they call it a darkroom.

But I pause.

A giggle in the corner.

I turn and realize I am shivering. Why is it so cold?

A laugh, behind me.

The cold is piercing, an icicle down my spine, I breathe it in, feel it pinch my nostrils, settle in my lungs. All the weight in my body has sunk into my feet. I cannot move, even as the air chills around my neck, clutches at my throat. I stare.

I can almost see it.

Red eyes, glowing in the dark.

A metallic scrape –

I whirl about – expecting –

Jarrett throws open the curtains and my eyes dart across the room. But nothing.

Not in the light.

♀

After I tell them of the laughter in the darkroom, the eyes, the boys set off on their own excursion. Veronica takes my hand and leads me to the bedroom. I am still shivering. She pats my hand as if I'm a Victorian hysteric, and I half expect her to pull smelling salts out of her bosom. Instead, she pulls out a toke and lights up.

She offers, but I decline. I've had enough spooks for the night. Her hands press into my back as she murmurs, *you're tight*, her fingers push and release, like a cat kneading its cushion. Her breath on the back of my neck as she works my shoulders.

This is not relaxing.

I think I'll just go to sleep, I say.

Veronica opens her bags and hands me silk panties and a thin camisole, translucent in this evening light. *Try them on*, she says, fiddling with her camera lens, and I remember my bag, safely stowed in the trunk of my abandoned car, on the bridge above the river.

I am wet with desire, wet since I first saw her, so I say, turn around, knowing my juices have been seeping out of me, ashamed of the tell-tale stain. She turns with careless grace. I fumble with my clothes and hold her undergarments in front of me.

But I wear boxer shorts, I say.

Veronica only laughs.

She's been in these, I think, as I slither into silkiness. Tight, for I am bigger than her. Every movement is a caress and I want to touch myself, this fabric, so much like a stroking tease, so close against the skin. The camisole glides over my breasts and I am in torment.

Veronica turns, appraises me. *Good*, she says, amused. *You must be cold*, and she glances down at my hardening nipples. Exposed, I climb into bed, under the sheets. I watch her as she undresses, how snugly her panties fit her, that tantalizing V, eyes drawn to her pubic hair. She leans, and I can see the curve of her ass, gliding into where her cunt would be. Her breasts are pert, with a certain insouciance. Topless, Veronica sits by the window, flicks the ash into a tray, lies back and closes her eyes.

If she's asleep I can ride the pillows. . . .

She turns off the light.

I can see the light burning from her cigarette.

I close my eyes.

The sheets lie heavy against my skin and every cell in my body feels alive. How like a hand those silk clinging panties. I toss and turn, throw off the comforter, the sheet.

Veronica sits in the dark, watching. The glowing ember tells me she is still there. All the darkness of the room seems to emanate from those eyes, and her lips, I am sure, are curled into a sardonic smile. The air is thick with sweetness. The bed is soft, the pillows yielding. But I want the comfort of her fingers deep inside me, her bite marks on my ass. Somehow, I think she knows this, and waits, as the moonlight falls over my parted thighs. She does not move, but I can feel her heart pacing, stalking in the shadows. I close my eyes and fall – into what, I do not know.

♀

I wake in darkness and turn on the light. Veronica is not beside me. Veronica is not in the room. I think of Jarrett with a flash of hatred and skulk out of the chamber. In the hallway, I hear them. Low animal grunts. Uninhibited rutting passion.

In the dining hall I make a cup of lapsong souchong. I swallow, smell the smoky aroma of the tea, think of Veronica and try to unclench my cunt. What does it matter, I say to myself, what do I care? I peel a lichee, pop the tangy fruit into my mouth, spit out the hard, oval seed. I look over the heart–shaped persimmons, ripe–orange close to cinnabar. The flesh is succulent, gives easily under my pressure, and how like a cunt its texture.

I walk to the boys' room, peer through the keyhole.

But it is Martin splayed on the bed, Jarrett riding him, their contrasting bodies fitting together so perfectly, their movements in time. I stare at their beauty, but it is Veronica that I want. I wander through the halls, up the staircase, into rooms with furniture covered in white sheets. Moonlight gives them a ghostly countenance and I shiver.

I come to the balcony of the dome, the music room below. I look and scream.

Veronica, on the studio floor, body twisted, dead eyes glazed.

♀

I race downstairs. My shouts bring Martin and Jarrett and we scramble into the music room. I brace myself for the sight of Veronica, shattered and bloodied, her mouth struck open, silent.

The body is not what I expect.

The cello, smashed, lies scattered in pieces at the centre of the room. The strings are shredded and even the bow is snapped neatly in two. Jarrett groans, staggers back to the wall. We can only stand and stare.

Veronica, I think, where is Veronica?

Jarrett tries to gather up the shattered pieces but it is hopeless. His trembling hands hold the splintered neck. He cries, a painfull sound from such a proud man.

Jarrett, I offer, hopelessly. He brushes me away.

His cello. His beautiful, beloved cello.

Martin has stumbled into the sculpting studio. His mouth works, jaws moving without a sound. He points.

A broken torso, in marble. Unmistakably Martin. His head crushed. The stone is polished, impossibly finished, weeks, no, months of work completed within hours, such gruesome detail.

I am cold, very cold.

Martin takes Jarrett's hand. Let's get out of here. He tugs and Jarrett follows.

I am alone.

Martin's right, I think, get out while you can.

But Veronica. . . .

I go to the darkroom, through the veil of curtains. I snap on the red light and see the space in scarlet hue. Titian, I think, but push this from my mind. The tap drips, metronymic. The trays sit by the wall. In the last tray, floating just below the surface, a sheet developing, an image becoming.

I gaze.

On the sheet, darkness deepens, a flush of silver nitrate, uncertain at first, the blurred edges, lines unfurl, shadows pushing up, like a conjurer's trick. The image takes form.

I gape. Impossible.

The photograph: a woman, legs spread open, Veronica's mouth on the woman's clitoris as her fingers slide inside of her cunt, a wet, silver sheen of labia, hips raised, belly taut, muscles straining towards that rush, neck, a sinewy cord, a face contorted with desire, with need. A face. My face.

Impossible.

I step back, the blood beating at the back of my eyes. Behind me, on the drying line, hang a thousand images of desire, framing me with shocking intimacy. And Veronica, always Veronica.

But I don't believe, not in devils, nor angels. The earth spins around the sun, as the stars fan out into infinite space. There are no demons, no destinies, no fate. Fairy tales are fairy tales, and no amount of thunderous clapping can bring back the dead.

I realize this story is mine to make. I choose the forking paths. My car waits on the bridge, my life in the city. I can retrace my steps, walk back into the waking world, out of this nightmare –

♀

But I stay, entrapped by the promise of a photograph.

♀

I feel her hands encircle my waist, slinking down, cupping my mound. A caress so light that I hold the whimper in my throat. Her fingers play over my ass as she easily rips the silk away, and I shiver at her casual strength. My wetness exposed, she hunts me down, the length of back, to the hidden folds, stinging kisses, and rasping, rapacious tongue. Does she hear the hum in my blood, sniff out my clumsy longing? Her nails claw my thighs, the purr of her lips as she tastes me, a toying, teasing play. Tongue so quick, a nuzzling murmur, her breath, a touch in my cunt. She slides inside, opens me, so deliciously, and yes, I have wanted her there, craved her inside of me, each thrust of her splitting me open, my body inscribed, enfolded, she fucks, as if to tear me inside-out, bites into the back of my neck, besplattering the page, marking me as her own, my lover, my elusive vampire cat.

Tamai Kobayashi was born in Japan and raised in Canada. She is the author of *All Names Spoken* (co-authored with Mona Oikawa, Sister Vision Press, 1992) and *Exile and the Heart* (Women's Press, 1998), and is also a film and videomaker, screenwriter, and songwriter. She lives in Toronto.

Dear Reader:

I hope you have enjoyed this collection of erotic short stories. If I may say, in my own defence, that these stories are, of course, fantasies and fictions and no names have been changed to protect the not-so-innocent. My inspirations have been varied. The Vampire Cat appears in Japanese folktales, as does the Yuki Onna. Cinderella and Red Riding Hood also appear in this collection, albeit disguised, as does the Chekovian kiss. Caliban reclaims the title of beast and steals the beauty, Miranda, from a Bluebeardesque father. Hoffman joins the electronic age, but as always, her Olympia is not all that she seems (of course, she's even more). Although the usual suspects do appear (the voyeur, the threesome, the requisite orgy), I hope these stories hold some surprises. All in all, there is an eclectic cast of characters. I hope you've found this collection to be both quixotic and erotic.

Dear Reader, these are stories, perhaps seductions, but stories can subvert and still amuse (the Vampyr is a cynic, after all). Remember, if you don't like the ending, change it.